HEARTS IN THE WIND

What Reviewers Say About MJ Williamz's Work

Exposed

"The love affair between Randi and Eleanor goes along in fits and starts. It is a wonderful story, and the sex is hot. Definitely read it as soon as you have a chance!"—Janice Best, Librarian (Albion District Library)

Shots Fired

"MJ Williamz, in her first romantic thriller, has done an impressive job of building the tension and suspense. Williamz has a firm grasp of keeping the reader guessing and quickly turning the pages to get to the bottom of the mystery. *Shots Fired* clearly shows the author's ability to spin an engaging tale and is sure to be just the beginning of great things to follow as the author matures." —*Lambda Literary Review*

"Williamz tells her story in the voices of Kyla, Echo, and Detective Pat Silverton. She does a great job with the twists and turns of the story, along with the secondary plot. The police procedure is first rate, as are the scenes between Kyla and Echo, as they try to keep their relationship alive through the stress and mistrust." —*Just About Write*

Forbidden Passions

"*Forbidden Passions* is 192 pages of bodice ripping antebellum erotica not so gently wrapped in the moistest, muskiest pantalets of lesbian horn dog high jinks ever written. While the book is joyfully and unabashedly smut, the love story is well written and the characters are multi-dimensional. …*Forbidden Passions* is the very model of modern major erotica, but hidden within the sweet swells and trembling clefts of that erotica is a beautiful May–September romance between two wonderful and memorable characters."—*Rainbow Reader*

Sheltered Love

"The main pair in this story is astoundingly special, amazingly in sync nearly all the time, and perhaps the hottest twosome on a sexual front I have read to date. …This book has an intensity plus an atypical yet delightful original set of characters that drew me in and made me care for most of them. Tantalizingly tempting!" —*Rainbow Book Reviews*

Speakeasy

"*Speakeasy* is a bit of a blast from the past. It takes place in Chicago when Prohibition was in full flower and Al Capone was a name to be feared. The really fascinating twist is a small speakeasy operation run by a woman. She was more than incredible. This was such great fun and I most assuredly recommend it. Even the bloody battling that went on fit with the times and certainly spiced things up!"—*Rainbow Book Reviews*

"In the Bell Tower" in *Women of the Dark Streets*

"New Orleans and a sexy female vampire helps an awkward visitor blossom and make sweet, sweet love all night long. Delicious!" —*Rainbow Book Reviews*

Heartscapes

"The development of the relationship was well told and believable. Now the sex actually means something and M J Williamz certainly knows how to write a good sex scene. Just when you think life has finally become great again for Jesse, Odette has a stroke and can't remember her at all. It is heartbreaking. Odette was a lovely character and I thought she was well developed. She was just the right person at the right time for Jesse. It was an engaging book, a beautiful love story."—*Inked Rainbow Reads*

By the Author

Shots Fired

Forbidden Passions

Initiation by Desire

Speakeasy

Escapades

Sheltered Love

Summer Passion

Heartscapes

Love on Liberty

Love Down Under

Complications

Lessons in Desire

Hookin' Up

Score

Exposed

Broken Vows

Model Behavior

Scene of the Crime

Thief of the Heart

Desires After Dark

Hearts in the Wind

Hearts in the Wind

by

MJ Williamz

2023

HEARTS IN THE WIND

ISBN 13: 978-1-63679-288-0

This Trade Paperback Original Is Published By
Bold Strokes Books, Inc.
P.O. Box 249
Valley Falls, NY 12185

First Edition: January 2023

Credits
Editor: Cindy Cresap
Production Design: Susan Ramundo
Cover Design By Tammy Seidick

Acknowledgments

As always, I start by thanking my awesome wife, Laydin Michaels, for her love, support, and inspiration.

I'd also like to thank all the folks at Bold Strokes Books for continuing to believe in me and giving me the platform to tell my stories.

Special thanks to my beta readers, Sarah and Sue.

And a huge thank you to you, the readers. Without you, I couldn't continue to do this.

Dedication

To everyone who keeps reading my books.
This one is for you.

CHAPTER ONE

Fuck, it's hot." Beth Richards placed her head under the spigot and let the water flow over her. For once, she was grateful for her fine hair. It was soaked in no time. Feeling much better, she stood, put her straw cowboy hat back in place, and got in the truck. She still had to go check on the mamas and calves in the other pasture.

As she crossed the property, she wondered not for the first time how much longer she'd be able to keep the farm afloat. Her grandpappy had farmed this land and then her father before her. Her dad had died suddenly from an aneurysm a few years back, and Beth had been doing her level best to keep her head above water. It wasn't easy. And it was getting harder with each passing day.

She finished her morning chores and went back to the farmhouse. At least she'd been able to keep it in good shape. She'd reroofed it the year before to stop the leaks and had given it a fresh coat of paint the year before that. It was cute. She seldom took the time to look at it, really see it, but she was in a nostalgic mood that day. She thought back to her childhood days in that house when they'd visited Grandpappy and Meemaw. She couldn't fight the smile. Those had been wonderful days.

Beth let herself into the mudroom and heard her mama call out, "Who's there?"

"It's me, Mama. Beth."

She stepped, bootless, into the kitchen to see her mom and her little sister, Kelsey, sitting at the small table.

"Who are you?" Mama said. "What are you doing in my house?"

Her voice trembled with a combination of indignance and fear.

"Mama?"

Kelsey shook her head.

"She's having a bad day."

Mama had been diagnosed with Alzheimer's two years prior. Beth and Kelsey cared for her together, having promised each other Mama would die at home. The bulk of the responsibility fell to Kelsey since Beth was so busy with the farm.

Beth nodded solemnly and sat down next to Mama. She took her cold, frail hands in her own.

"It's me, Mama. Beth. Your firstborn." There was no flash of recognition in Mama's eyes, but at least she stopped trembling. "Y'all hungry? I could fix us some breakfast."

Kelsey shot up.

"I'll go to Vernon and pick up some kolaches."

Beth started to object, but Kelsey was already out the door. Beth couldn't begrudge her sister wanting to get away. Caring for their mama was a suffocating weight. And Vernon, the closest real town, was only fifteen minutes away. There was no place to buy kolaches in their tiny town of Walker.

So Beth sat with her mama and struggled to take her mind off the worries of the farm and focus on her mother's needs.

"Can I get you a cup of coffee?" said Beth.

"Yes, please. Just a little cream and sugar."

Beth didn't know whether to laugh or cry. Mama had taken her coffee the same way for as long as Beth had been alive. There was no reason to tell Beth how to make her coffee. But Beth was fairly certain her mom still wasn't sure who she was.

She poured them each a cup of coffee then sat back down. Her mama had picked up the paper and started reading it.

"I don't understand anything anymore." Mama threw down the paper.

"What don't you understand? Let me help you."

"Any of it. I don't understand any of it."

She was getting agitated, and Beth knew she would have to work to deescalate her. She picked up the paper.

"Let's start at the front page. Here. Tell me what you want me to explain to you." She made sure not to sound as irritated as she felt.

"What's Corvid?" she said.

"Corvid?" Beth craned her neck to see what Mama was looking at. "Oh, Covid. That's the pandemic."

Mama stared at her blankly. Beth didn't know how many times she'd tried to explain this, but one more time wouldn't hurt.

"It's the pandemic. Lots of people have died from it. Remember when we took you to get your shots?"

The light seemed to go on in Mama's head.

"That mess that's going around?"

"Yes," Beth said. "That mess that's going around."

Mama nodded solemnly.

"That's terrible that people are still dying. I'm not going to die, am I?"

Beth felt her eyes grow wet.

"No, Mama," she said. "That's why we all got our shots."

Mama got up to get another cup of coffee. Beth marveled again at how normal Mama could seem and yet how lost in her mind she truly was.

"How are the crops?" she said.

"Looking good. We should be able to harvest cotton in the next couple of months and the pumpkins will be ready to sell by October."

"You work so hard, Bethy. Too hard for a girl. We need a man to run this place."

Beth's neck hairs bristled. She knew Mama meant well, but she was tired of hearing she couldn't keep the farm afloat by herself. Part of this was how true it rang to her as she was filled with self-doubt. She didn't need Mama feeding her own neurosis. She took a deep breath and calmed herself before she answered.

"We don't need a stranger running this farm. It's our farm and I can take care of it the way Daddy and Grandpappy did."

"You work too hard. You should find a nice man and get married. Let your husband run the farm."

Marriage was not on Beth's radar. She wasn't against it per se, she just didn't have the time it took to meet someone and develop any kind of relationship with them. Besides, she had no interest at all in any of Walker's eligible bachelors.

Beth set her coffee cup in the dishwasher and stood still. She heard a car approaching. She tensed. Who could it be? Then she remembered Kelsey had gone for kolaches and was probably just getting home.

Buddy, Beth's pit pointer mix started barking fiercely. The car stopped in front of the house instead of on the side where Kelsey would have parked. Beth looked out the front window. She saw a gold Mercedes. No one she knew drove a gold Mercedes. Or any other color for that matter.

"What the actual fuck?" she mumbled as she watched the car door open.

Out stepped a tall blond woman in skinny black jeans tucked into black boots. Which had heels. Boots with heels? Beth was on edge. The woman also wore a pink Izod shirt and a black felt cowboy hat. Nobody in their right mind wore a felt hat in this heat. Who the hell was this and what did she want?

❖

What fresh hell was this? Evelyn Bremer pulled into the tiny town of Walker, Texas. She was used to small towns and the people who inhabited them. She saw them all the time in her line of business. But this tiny west Texas town had a population of three hundred and twenty and was barely a blip on the road.

Evelyn exhaled. She longed for her comfortable condo in Dallas. But this was business. She had a job to do and she was damned good at her job. She'd be in and out of this town in a day or so.

She turned south at the only traffic light in town. She drove past cattle ranches and small farms growing cotton, oats, and rye. At least the area surrounding the Podunk town was pretty. There was lots of green and the rolling hills were lovely. The crosswind made it hard to keep her car on the road, but that only made her smile. Wind. It was what she lived for.

Evelyn pulled off the paved road and onto a dirt road that took her to a cute farmhouse. It was painted pale yellow with light blue accents. It looked to be in good shape. Unlike the farm. Evelyn had done her research and knew the farm was struggling. She'd wave one hundred thousand dollars in front of a Mrs. Ida Richards and it would be all over. She smiled. Easy peasy.

She parked her car and got out, looking around as she stretched. This place was perfect. She had to have it. And Evelyn never took no for an answer.

She heard a dog barking inside the house and wondered what breed she'd be dealing with this time. She kept dog treats in her purse for occasions such as this. She could warm the heart of any dog. She just hoped she could warm the heart of Ida as well. She put on her best smile and climbed the steps of the wraparound porch. She raised her hand to knock when the door was opened and a woman who looked a bit like a drowned rat stepped outside.

"What do you want?" the rat said.

"Hi there," Evelyn drawled. "I'm here to see a Mrs. Ida Richards?"

"What do you want with her?"

Evelyn wanted to tower over this impudent woman and demand to speak to Mrs. Richards, but she kept the forced smile glued in place.

"I have a business proposition for her."

"She's not interested."

"Please. It's important I speak to her," said Evelyn.

"Well, you can't." The drowned rat turned her back and reached for the front door. Without conscious thought, Evelyn reached out and grabbed her arm.

"Please. Why can't I speak to her? It'll only take a moment."

"Mama's got Alzheimer's," said Beth. "You'll only upset her. And I won't let you do that."

"I'm so sorry," Evelyn said, and she meant it. She'd heard horror stories of that disease. "May I ask your relationship to Mrs. Richards?"

"I'm her daughter."

The rat's sky blue eyes were still hard and unwelcoming, but Evelyn knew she'd handled tougher customers.

"I'm Evelyn." She extended her hand. "But you can call me Evie."

"Evelyn." She acted like she was trying to decide if she liked the name. Evelyn fought not to laugh. "I'm Beth."

She didn't take the extended hand. Her gaze never wavered. It held Evelyn's in a combination of contempt and disdain.

"Let's sit down, Beth. I'd like to talk to you."

"I'm not interested. Look, I'm sorry you drove out here for nothing, but that's what you're getting from me. Why don't you take your fancy car and get the hell out of here."

"At least hear me out," said Evelyn. "If you're still not interested, I'll drive off into the sunset."

"You're wasting your time. And mine. I've got work to do."

"Please, sit."

Beth looked from Evelyn to the wicker chairs and back to Evelyn.

"Let me go check on Mama. You can sit down. I'll be out when I can."

"Fair enough," Evelyn said as the door slammed shut in her face.

She sat in a chair and surveyed the small farm. She could make so much money off it. She had to have it. As she sat there, an old Ford F-250 pulled up and parked on the side of the house. Shortly after the truck arrived, Beth was back out front. She held out a bag to Evelyn.

"Kolache?"

"Why thank you." Kolaches were not on Evelyn's fairly strict diet, but she took a sausage one as kind of a peace offering.

Beth sat in the chair next to her but didn't say another word. She seemed to be lost in thought as she chewed her breakfast. Evelyn was loathe to interrupt but wanted to get down to business.

"Penny for your thoughts?"

"Don't know that they're worth that much."

Evelyn was growing tired of this Beth character. She wanted to seal the deal and move on to her next venture.

"Beth?" said Evelyn.

"Hm?"

"Have you ever thought of selling this place?"

"Nope." It was said without a moment's hesitation.

"It's not doing very well."

"Fuck you. I work my ass off and we're doing just fine."

Beth's eyes were hard like slate. Her response was immediate, visceral. Evelyn realized she had her work cut out for her.

"I'd very much like you to sell the farm to me. I'm prepared to make you a very generous offer."

"It's not for sale. Now get the hell out of here."

Beth went inside, slamming the door behind her.

Chapter Two

Beth fumed the rest of the day. How dare that city slicker waltz onto her porch and think Beth's family farm was for sale? Yes, Beth had been struggling to make ends meet, but she was keeping her head above water. Barely, but still. She didn't need some highfalutin, egocentric, wannabe coming out to her farm thinking she'd sell it. Especially one who didn't even know how to dress right. Ugh.

Her stomach had soured so she hadn't finished breakfast or eaten lunch. Every time she thought of Evelyn her blood boiled. She fed the cattle their wet food that evening then went in and took a shower.

"Where do you think you're going?" Kelsey glared at Beth.

"I've had a rough day. I'm going to town to get some dinner and grab a drink."

"Oh no you don't."

"What do you mean?" Beth felt her blood pressure rising. "Mama's in bed. You won't have to do anything. I just need to get out of here."

"I've been with Mama all day. I'm exhausted. I need to go to town. I need to burn off some energy."

"You mean you need to get laid." Kelsey's extracurriculars disgusted Beth.

"Exactly."

"Think about Mama. Your reputation in Vernon is widespread. Everyone knows you're a slut."

"I'm not a slut. Just because you're a thirty-two-year-old virgin. I have needs. And I'm going to town."

Beth watched in dismay as Kelsey took the truck keys and slammed the back door behind her.

"Shit." She reached under the kitchen cabinet for her good sipping tequila and poured herself two fingers. She stepped down into the den and sat in the old, brown leather recliner with its innards popping out of various holes.

While the outside of the house was in good shape, what lay within was definitely not. Beth had so much work to do to. She opened her phone and began making a list of supplies she'd need from Vernon to start getting the inside of the house as nice as the outside.

Beth heard the tell-tale sound of her mother's walker.

"Mama?"

Her mom appeared in the dining room.

"Where's my luggage?" said Mama.

"What luggage is that?"

"I need to go home. Where's my luggage?"

This was the last thing Beth needed right then, but she took a deep breath and decided to try to redirect.

"Mama? Did you have a dream? What woke you up?"

Redirection did not work. Mama grew agitated.

"I woke up because it's time to go home. Now tell me where my luggage is. I have clothes to pack."

Beth got up to meet her mom in the dining room, but Mama had other ideas. She tried to step down into the den, lost her footing, and face-planted on the carpet.

"Mama? Are you okay?"

"Help me up."

Beth was already standing over her. She helped her to a sitting position. Then pulled Mama, who only weighed a hundred pounds, to her feet. Beth assessed her and decided that a couple of rug burns on her cheek were the worst of the damage.

"How are your ribs?" she asked.

"My what?"

"Take a deep breath for me, Mama."

Mama took a deep breath.

"I'm fine."

"Yeah. You seem to be. Let's get you back to bed."

She followed her mom down the hall and to her bedroom. When Mama was all tucked in, Beth went back to the den to finish her drink. What a royally fucked day she'd had. Thank God tomorrow would be a new day.

The following morning, Beth came in from the fields and found Kelsey scrambling eggs for breakfast.

"What's the occasion?" said Beth.

"Does there have to be an occasion?"

"For you to cook? Yes. Oh, never mind. You went to town last night. No wonder you're in such a good mood."

"No," Kelsey said. "It's not like that. I did meet someone, but not the way you're thinking."

"Color me curious," said Beth.

"I met a woman."

"There's a twist."

"Not like that," said Kelsey. "But she was really cool. She's from Dallas. Her name is Evie."

"Not the fake blond city slicker?"

"The very same. Yeah, she mentioned you two didn't exactly hit it off."

"Not even close. I hope I never see her again."

Buddy started barking and Beth heard tires on the gravel. Who could that be?

"Speaking of her…" Kelsey took the pan off the stove and headed to the front door.

"Damn you, Kelsey!"

"Language," said Mama.

"Sorry. But this woman wants to buy the farm."

"Pappy won't sell the farm."

"No," Beth sighed. "Pappy won't."

She opened the back door to sneak out.

"Beth? Where are you going?" Just the sound of Evelyn's voice made Beth's skin crawl. "I thought we were having a family breakfast."

"You're not in the family."

"Bethy?" said Mama. "Why are you upset?"

The fact that her mother didn't remember the conversation they'd just had frustrated Beth further. Not the fact that Mama couldn't remember. She couldn't help it and Beth would never hold that against her. Just the fact that Beth wanted her as an ally.

"I'm upset that Kelsey invited a stranger into our house."

"She looks lovely."

"Looks can be deceiving."

"Relax, Beth," Evelyn said. "I'm just here for breakfast. Kelsey and I had more fun last night. We're like sisters now."

"Let's get a few things straight. You're not her sister. You're not part of our family. And you'll never own this farm."

"Turbo down, Beth," said Kelsey. "Have you heard her offer?"

"Fu—" Beth remembered her mama. "I don't give a rip about her offer. The farm is not for sale. Now, if you'll excuse me, I've got work to do."

"Please sit down." Evelyn's brown eyes pleaded with her. "We won't talk about whether or not the farm is for sale again this morning."

Beth sat and pushed her eggs around on her plate. She was nauseous. Being in Evelyn's presence seemed to bring out the worst in her. When Kelsey served the bacon and the biscuits made from Meemaw's recipe, Beth couldn't deny her appetite. She inhaled the food and simply tuned out Evelyn and Kelsey.

She finished and encouraged Mama to eat some more so she could take her meds. Beth got her mom medicated and walked with her to the sunroom to sit on the chaise lounge. Beth watered the plants then sat down and read to Mama from *Gone With The Wind*. It was her Mama's favorite book.

"You'll do anything to avoid Evie, won't you?" Kelsey poked her head in.

"I just wanted to spend some time with Mama."

"You just want an excuse to go to town tonight."

"I think I've earned it."

"Whatever. Do what you need."

❖

Evie had enjoyed her time with Kelsey that morning, but she knew she'd already won her over. Beth was the hard sell and she hadn't had time to really talk to her. She needed to find a way to break through that tough exterior and connect with the woman hiding behind it. But how?

After breakfast, Evie had picked up more supplies for the Airbnb. Wine, peanuts, notebooks, pens, and a new flash drive were strewn across the dining room table. Evie had spent the rest of the day reviewing numbers. How much could she realistically offer Beth? She was offering market value, and Kelsey seemed on board, but Beth would require more. It was Evie's job to figure just how high she could go.

After deciding she could go a little over market value, she texted her business partner and let him know her plans. Her phone rang almost as soon as she'd hit send.

"Robert?" She answered. "Don't bust my balls over this."

"That's too high! Are you out of your mind?"

"I assure you I know what I'm doing."

"We should shove fifty at her and shove her out the door."

The hair on the back of Evie's neck stood up.

"It's not that easy."

"Why the fuck not? That farm is about to go belly up. Any money we give her she should be happy to take."

"She's proud," said Evie.

"Oh, no," said Robert.

"What?"

"Did you sleep with her?"

"What? No. Of course not."

"Evie..."

"I swear Robert. Look. Let me handle this, okay? Trust me."

"I do, Evie. But I want wind turbines up there and I want them up within a year. Make this happen."

"That's what I want too. It'll happen. Good-bye, Robert."

Restless and on edge, Evie decided to go for a walk. She put on khaki capris and a light green Izod shirt, slipped into her OluKai sandals, and set out down Main Street. It was a balmy ninety degrees and, while she was used to heat, she was also used to air conditioning and told herself she'd stop at the first bar-type place she came to.

Three blocks later, she was standing in front of a dive called Catfish Charlie's. She didn't care, as long as it had air conditioning. Bracing herself for country music and rednecks, she opened the heavy oak door and stepped in.

She stopped for a moment just inside to let her eyes adjust to the darkness. She saw a jukebox along the far wall to her right and about ten tables in the middle with four booths lining the outside wall. Red seemed to be the theme, from the booths to the tablecloths to the giant catfish head sticking out above the bar that ran along the inner wall.

Three people were sitting at the bar and didn't seem to pay her any attention, so she walked over and sat at the far end of the bar. An older gentleman whose age she couldn't guess, wandered over.

"What can I get for you?"

"Something cold and wet, please."

He threw his head back and laughed.

"Now, that I can do. What's your poison?"

"Captain Morgan. I don't care what you mix it with. Surprise me."

The bartender meandered away, and Evie spun on her barstool to survey the other half of the establishment. There were more tables on the other side of the bar which appeared to have place settings.

"Here's your apple crisp. Enjoy." The bartender set the drink in front of her.

"Thank you. Do you serve food here?"

"Damned straight."

Evie's stomach growled and she realized she'd been so full from breakfast she had skipped lunch.

"May I see a menu, please?"

"Of course. Since you seem like you may stick around, I'll let you know, I'm Charlie. You need anything at all, pretty lady, you just ask old Charlie."

"As in Catfish Charlie?"

"The very one." He placed the menu on the bar. "I'll be taking your order, as well. Just let me know when you're ready."

"Thank you." She afforded him her best smile. After all, he thought she was pretty.

Evie perused the menu and thought she'd never seen so much fried food anywhere except maybe the Texas State Fair. Frog legs and catfish were just the beginning. She finally found the salad menu and ordered the chef. That should hold her.

She had just finished her salad and ordered a second drink when she was blinded by the light the front door let in. The door quickly closed and she turned back toward the bar, looking in the mirror to see who the newcomer was.

Holy shit. It was Beth Richards. Their gazes met in the mirror and Beth's eyes widened then narrowed. She made a point of moving to the other end of the bar. The two men down there greeted her by name.

"I'll have a rusty nail. Neat," Beth said.

"Already got it for you." Charlie handed her the drink. "How're you holding up?"

Evie had been watching the exchange with mild curiosity. Now her ears perked up. Once again, Beth met her gaze in the mirror before looking away and smiling at Charlie.

"We're doing great, Charlie. Everything is running smoothly."

"Bullshit," Evie mumbled into her drink. "Utter and complete bullshit."

CHAPTER THREE

Beth couldn't shake the tightness in her gut. Evelyn Bremer was the last person she wanted to see when she went into town to unwind. The fucking bitch was stalking her. Hanging out and ingratiating herself with Kelsey, showing up at the house for breakfast, and now in Beth's favorite watering hole. What a psychotic bitch.

She was about to take the last swallow of her drink when Charlie walked up with another one.

"Sorry, Charlie, but I'm on my way out."

Charlie smiled at her.

"Courtesy of the beautiful stranger at the end of the bar."

"Like I said, I was just leaving."

"I'd like to consider it a peace offering."

How had Beth not seen Evelyn walk up in the mirror? She'd been too focused on Charlie.

"Not interested." Beth turned to go. Evelyn grabbed her arm.

"Just one drink. We can talk about anything you like. Anything but the farm."

"No farm talk?" Beth was suspicious.

"No farm talk."

"Fine. Thanks for the drink." She knew her voice was cold and her tone flat, but she didn't care. Even after a free drink, she didn't like Evelyn and nothing was going to change that.

"Tell me about yourself," said Evelyn.

"What do you want to know?"

"I don't know. Anything. Are you seeing someone?"

"Not at the moment. You?"

"I'm free and easy."

Beth didn't doubt the easy part. That was probably why Evelyn and Kelsey had hit it off so well.

"There aren't a lot of men here. So, you'd better hurry home to whatever city you came from." Evelyn threw her head back and laughed. Beth was confused. What had she said that was so hilarious? "I'm not sure what I said that was so funny."

"Men, Beth. You said men. That's what made me laugh. I have no interest in men."

"Who do you have interest in?"

"Women."

Beth pondered that for a while. She'd heard of women loving women, but had never actually met a lesbian before. She nodded. "Got it."

"And you, Beth? Which team do you play for?"

Beth thought long and hard before answering. She didn't want to offend Evelyn, though she wasn't quite sure why not.

"I'm too busy running the farm to play for any team."

"I believe that." Evelyn raised her glass. "To hard work."

Although Beth doubted Evelyn had ever worked hard in her life, she clinked her glass.

"To hard work indeed." She stared into her half empty glass and decided what the hell? Who cared if she offended Evelyn? "Although I doubt you know what hard work is."

Evelyn laughed again. Beth was growing more irritated by the moment. Why the fuck did Evelyn laugh at everything she said.

"I work very hard," said Evelyn. "Harder than you can imagine."

"I don't believe you. After all, you left whatever city you live in to come out here and harass my family and me. Seems to me if you were a hard worker, you'd be in your office doing whatever you do."

"Dallas."

"What?"

"Whatever city I live in? I live in Dallas. Have you ever been there?"

"I have. I go there for livestock auctions. But I'm not going to talk any more about the farm." She downed the rest of her drink. "Thanks again for the drink. Hopefully I won't be seeing you around."

Beth was a jumble of emotions as she drove home. She was angry at herself for taking that drink and irritated at Evelyn for everything. Just being herself drove Beth to the brink. She tried not to think of Evelyn as she got close to the house, but that proved futile. Evelyn was dangerous. She could sense it in every ounce of her being. She truly hoped she'd seen the last of her.

The first thing Beth did when she got home was check on Mama. But she wasn't in bed where she should have been. She called for her. No answer. She entered Mama's room and found her in the adjoining bathroom. Mama was face down on the floor and not moving.

"Mama?" Beth called. She wanted to shake her and try to wake her, but didn't know if she'd injure her further. Instead she called 9-1-1.

The approaching ambulance woke Kelsey.

"What's going on?"

"Mama fell. She's unconscious." Beth fought to keep the edge out of her voice. It could have happened on anybody's watch. It just happened to fall on Kelsey's.

The ambulance rushed the still unconscious Mama to the hospital in Vernon. Kelsey and Beth followed in the truck. They arrived at the emergency room in time to see Mama's still body being wheeled inside.

"You can't come in," the nurse told Beth when she tried to enter.

"My mother has Alzheimer's. I need to be with her. When she comes to, she's going to be scared and confused. I need to be there."

The nurse stared at Beth as if sizing her up.

"Fine. But here." She handed Beth a mask.

Beth found Mama's bed.

"Who are you?" asked a man who looked to be just out of high school.

"Beth Richards. I'm her daughter. She has Alzheimer's. I need to be here."

"I'm Dr. Knox. Thanks for being here for her. They'll be taking her for a CT scan in just a moment so make yourself comfortable. She should be out soon."

The CT scan appeared normal according to Dr. Knox, but they'd know for sure after the radiologist read it. Mama finally came to. Kelsey bent over her.

"Mama. Thank God you're okay. We were so worried."

Beth watched Mama's eyes grow wide with terror as she looked around, clearly confused.

"Give her some space," said Beth.

"No. Mama? It's me. Kelsey. You had a fall that scared us."

"Where am I?"

"You're in the hospital."

"No," cried Mama. "That's where Pappy died. Get me out of here. I don't want to die!"

Beth pulled Kelsey back and gently took one of Mama's hands.

"It's okay. Sh. You're not going to die." She spoke in a quiet voice and tried to be as calming as she could. "We're going to take you home in just a minute. Okay?"

Mama's eyes focused on Beth. She nodded.

"Please take me home. Don't leave me here."

"We won't. I promise."

Dr. Knox examined Mama and declared she was fit to go home. Mama didn't seem to understand where they were going but was happy when Beth got her in her own bed.

❖

Evie groaned when her alarm went off at O-dark-thirty. She was tired and frustrated. And she hated this little Podunk town to which she'd exiled herself until the sale went through. Once she had the farmland, she would go back to Dallas and set things in motion to get the windmill farm built. Yes, she'd have to come back periodically over the next nine months or so to make sure things were going as planned, but she wouldn't have to get up at an ungodly hour to do so.

She was hoping to catch Beth unawares, off guard. Beth would likely be deep in work without an escape. She'd be an unwilling prisoner having no choice but to listen to Evie's spiel. At least Evie would be able to make an offer. She would give Beth something to think about. Instead of Beth simply saying no all the time. When Beth learned she would get over market value for the land alone, Evie was sure Beth would bite.

And, by catching Beth hard at work, she could play the work too hard card. Letting Beth know she understood and respected the amount of work it took to keep the farm going. And believing she should take the money and settle down somewhere. Maybe she could buy a little house in Walker. Or even Vernon. Not that it mattered to Evie what Beth did. As soon as her name was signed on the dotted line, she would never cross Evie's mind again.

The sun was just cresting the horizon when Evie pulled up in front of the soon to be demolished farmhouse. She smiled. Yes, it was cute and quaint and all those things, but it served no purpose to her. She couldn't wait until it was flattened.

Evie sat in her Mercedes wondering where she should start. The farm wasn't very large but it was spread out enough and Evie hadn't considered how to find Beth once she'd arrived. She decided that feeding the cattle would probably be first on Beth's agenda so drove along the rutted dirt road until she saw Beth's truck.

She parked her car and picked her way through the dirt and grass until she was behind Beth, who still hadn't sensed her. Beth was resting on the fence, chin on forearms. Evie walked up and stood next to her.

"You're hard at work already," said Evie.

"You should leave."

"Leave?" Evie gave Beth her best smile. "I just got here."

"You're not welcome here. I thought I made that clear."

"But, last night over drinks, I thought we had the start of a friendship."

"You thought wrong." Beth glared at Evie.

Evie took in the dark circles under Beth's bloodshot eyes.

"What the hell happened to you? You look like you've been rode hard and put away wet, as they say."

"Late night. Rough night."

"Where did you go after you left Charlie's?"

Beth shoved off from the fence and yanked some more hay out of her truck.

"I came home."

"And?" Evie couldn't explain why she was so curious, but she was.

Beth tossed the hay over the fence.

"If you must know, Mama fell last night. We were at the hospital with her."

"Oh, Beth." Evie was sincere. "I'm so sorry to hear that. I hope she's okay."

"As okay as an Alzheimer's patient can be. She wasn't hurt seriously if that's what you mean."

"It's got to be so hard. Running the farm and taking care of her."

"Kelsey helps."

"Have you considered getting caregivers coming in to help?" said Evie.

"I don't need no strangers taking care of my mama. We do just fine."

"I can help, Beth. I know you think I'm the enemy but I can really help you all out."

"How? You going to sit with Mama all day? Read to her? Keep her mind stimulated? Check on her at night to make sure she hasn't fallen? Are you going to change her diapers when we get to that point?"

The bitterness and anger in Beth's words were hard to miss. Everything Beth said or did was done with an edge. She bit back rather than taking time to listen. It was time to make her really hear what Evie was trying to say.

"You know what I mean. I want to buy this property. Maybe you can get another farm. Maybe you could find a cute bungalow in town and live comfortably with your mom and Kelsey. Maybe you could go back to school. Learn a trade. You'd at least have options."

Beth whirled around and took a step toward Evie. Her hands were clenched at her side and her jaw muscles twitched.

"This was my grandpappy's farm. Then it was my pappy's. Now it's mine. Family. History. That's what's important to me. Not learning a new trade or moving into town or anything else your fucked up mind can dream up. I'm going to work this farm until my dying day."

Evie chose her next words carefully.

"Which would you rather? Lose it to the bank? Or sell it to me for just over market value?"

"Neither one is going to happen. Why don't you go back to Dallas and leave me the fuck alone? The bank can have this property over my dead body. And, when that happens, if you want to give them all that money for it, be my guest."

CHAPTER FOUR

Beth, why can't we discuss this like mature adults?"

Beth glared at Evie, her normally sky blue eyes as cloudy as a stormy sky.

"So now I'm not a mature adult? What the fuck? Why won't you just leave me alone?"

"Come to town with me. I'll buy you breakfast. We can talk."

Beth wheeled around and faced Evie.

"What part of 'I've got nothing to say to you' do you not understand?"

"Okay. You don't have to say anything," said Evie. "I'll do all the talking. You just have to listen. Really listen. Maybe ask a question or two. If you want. Only if you want. Please, Beth? Give me a chance."

"How the hell am I supposed to go to breakfast with you? I've got chores to do and then I've got to take care of Mama. Not everyone's life is as free and easy as yours."

Evie bristled at the comment. Her life could certainly appear free and easy, but she'd worked damned hard for her life. She'd fought demons Beth couldn't possibly imagine.

"Can your mom go to breakfast?"

"Hell, no. First of all, it would confuse the hell out of her. Secondly, there's a pandemic or have you not heard of that in Dallas?"

"I just thought I'd ask. Look. I'll go to the house and make sure your mom's taken care of. Doesn't Kelsey usually fix breakfast?"

"Only when she's picked up someone the night before."

"What?"

"Never mind. I don't need you to check on my mama. I'm perfectly capable of doing that. I have no desire to join you for breakfast. Why not take Kelsey?"

The idea of spending a little more time with the beautiful Kelsey was appealing for sure. But she wasn't the decision maker. Evie needed time with Beth.

"I want to talk to *you*. I need to talk to you. Please, Beth?"

Beth's shoulders drooped. She looked defeated and for a moment Evie felt sorry for her.

"Fine. Let me get cleaned up. I'll meet you at the Breakfast Barn in thirty."

"Can I trust you to be there?"

"Yeah. I'm doing this against my better judgment. Just for the record."

"Understood. I'll see you in a half hour then. And, Beth?"

"What?"

"Thank you."

"Don't thank me for jack," said Beth. "I'm not selling my farm to you. But I could use a good breakfast. I'll see you there."

She moseyed over to her truck and fired it up. Evie climbed into her car and turned it around. She smiled to herself as she drove into Vernon. This was huge. It was only a first step, but it was a huge first step. Meeting with Beth opened the door to her future. And she'd wooed tougher sells than Beth before.

Evie was feeling good as she parked her little Mercedes in among the trucks in front of the Breakfast Barn. She went in, found a booth, and perused the menu. Everything was covered in gravy. She put the menu down and looked at her watch. It had been forty-five minutes. Obviously, Beth wasn't going to show.

Frustrated and disappointed, Evie stepped out into the morning sun and almost collided with Beth.

"I didn't think you were coming," said Evie.

"Whatever. It took me a while to get my mama settled. If you don't want to do this, we can forget about it."

"Why forget about it? We're both here now. Let's see if we can survive each other's company through breakfast."

"I doubt it but I'm willing to try."

They had to wait for an empty table so Evie thought she'd try to get Beth to warm up to her.

"How's your mama doing this morning?"

"Not good." Beth exhaled heavily. "I felt bad leaving Kelsey there alone."

"I'm sure Kelsey can handle it."

"Oh, that's right. I forgot y'all were BFFs now."

"Are you jealous of your sister?" Evie said.

"What the fuck? Where did that come from? What's to be jealous of?"

"I don't know. I just sense some animosity and I'm just trying to find out where that comes from."

"We're siblings. There's supposed to be animosity. Are you an only child? Of course you are. That makes sense. Look. A table just emptied. Let's sit down."

Evie bit her tongue as she followed Beth to the table. The urge to lash out and rip this cocky country girl a new one was strong. She took a deep breath and slid into the booth across from Beth. If they both made it through breakfast alive it would be a miracle.

Beth finally set her menu down and looked at Evie.

"What do you want? I'm not selling the farm. End of story."

"Beth, listen to me. I've done my research. I know you're about to lose the farm. I'm offering to buy it from you. For significantly more than it's worth—"

"It's not for sale." It was said quietly, but the statement was full of venom. As if she dared Evie to bring it up again.

"We're talking significantly more than market value here."

Beth put her fingers in her ears.

"La la la la."

"Think of the care you could get for your mom with that kind of money."

"You leave my mama out of this. No one could care for her like I do."

"Kelsey could get her own place," Evie continued. "No more worrying about where she's been or who she's with. No more fighting all the time over who should care for Mama when."

"You don't understand family. Sure, we fight occasionally but we're always there for each other. That's what family is."

"Beth, you're a grown woman. Surely you want to settle down someday. Maybe start a family of your own. I can help you do that."

"And just how do you suggest I support myself? Farming is all I've known. It's all I've ever done. You want me to be a waitress here or something?"

"How about I throw in an education for you? Classes at Vernon College say."

Beth thought about what Evelyn was saying. Maybe she should go to school. Maybe she could get a desk job. She could buy a house in town and hire help for Mama. Help she so desperately needed. She shook her head. She couldn't, wouldn't sell the farm. That was her life.

"No. It's not going to happen," she said.

"Here comes our breakfast. Promise me you'll consider it."

"I won't."

Beth devoured her meal while Evelyn took one dainty bite at a time. Even the way she ate was annoying. She needed to get Evelyn out of town for good. But, how?

"What can I do to convince you to give up and get out of town?" said Beth.

"Sell me your house. I'm not leaving until we've signed on the dotted line. You want to get rid of me? Sell."

"So you're staying until hell freezes over?"

Evelyn smiled.

"I suppose I am."

"Great. Find someone else to harass in the meantime. Just leave me the fuck alone."

"No can do, I'm afraid. I need to buy your house."

"Why?"

"You really don't want to know," said Evelyn.

"Try me."

"I'm going to put up windmills on your property."

"Windmills? You want me to trade in my grandpappy's farm for windmills? You're special, aren't you?"

"Why not?"

"You don't understand. You can't. I'm leaving now. And now that I know what you want, I know you can give me a better number."

"I'm being very generous as it is."

"Think harder," said Beth. "Work your numbers again. I'll be waiting."

"Does that mean you'll actually consider selling to me?"

"I'm not making any promises. I'm just saying it's more likely if you sweeten the deal."

"Understood." Evelyn broke into a wide smile. "I'll rework the numbers."

"Yeah. You do that. Thanks for breakfast."

Beth left laughing to herself. Her farm wasn't worth anywhere near what Evelyn was offering her. She knew that. And she knew it would likely be foreclosed upon in the near future. She still didn't want to sell. But if Evelyn came up with more money, she might, just might, consider it. Besides, she had Mama to consider. Making some money off the farm would surely make it possible to get more help for her.

"About time you got home," Kelsey greeted her. "You took your sweet time in town."

"Where's Mama?"

"In bed. She feels like crap."

"I'm sure she's sore from her fall."

"I don't know, Beth. I think something's wrong."

"She was checked out last night. Nothing's broken."

"She's more confused than ever," said Kelsey.

"And you still let her take a nap? You know how disoriented she gets when she sleeps in the middle of the day."

"She wanted to go to bed. I'm not going to tell her no."

Beth went down the hall and found Mama sitting up on the edge of the bed.

"What's up, Mama?" she said.

"I want to go home."

That statement always hit Beth in the gut. This was the house Mama had grown up in. She'd lived here with Pappy. And now with Kelsey and herself.

"Mama," Beth said, "you are home."

"I'm not! I need to go home. Where's my luggage?"

"Mama, your luggage is in your closet. But, you don't need it."

Unshed tears shone in her eyes.

"How am I going to get all this home?"

"All what, Mama?" Beth kept her voice low and calm while the panic inside threatened to boil over.

"Everything. I brought all this with me and I need to take it home."

"Where's home?"

"I can't remember." She buried her face in her fragile hands.

"Would you like to go for a drive?"

"Where to?"

"Nowhere in particular. Let's just drive around."

"Will you take me home?"

"I'll take you wherever you want to go."

Beth knew there was no way Mama was going to get in the truck, so she got the car from the garage. She helped Mama in, buckled her seat belt for her, and took her into town.

She drove through the old neighborhoods where Mama had played as a child. She told her who used to live in which house, but Mama simply stared blankly at them.

"Do you remember the Smolniks? They used to live on the corner here. They had a pool?"

"I don't remember anything. Why can't I remember things?"

"It's the Alzheimer's, Mama."

"Can the doctor get rid of it for me?"

Beth fought not to cry.

"I'm sorry, Mama. There's no cure for it."

"Will you take me home then?"

"Of course."

Beth drove back to the farmhouse. She pulled to a stop in front of the wraparound porch.

"Where are we?" said Mama.

"We're home."

"No, we're not. I'm not getting out of this car. I don't know where you've taken me."

"Mama—"

"Only my daughters can call me that? Who are you?"

"It's me. Beth."

"No, you're not."

Beth sighed in relief when Kelsey came down the front steps and opened Mama's door. She reached around and unbuckled her.

"Who are you?" Mama looked so lost and confused.

"I live here," Kelsey said. "I just made some fresh lemonade. I thought you might be thirsty after your trip."

"I am parched. Thank you."

Kelsey helped Mama up the stairs. Beth put the car in the garage, hung her head, and cried.

CHAPTER FIVE

Evie called Robert as soon as she got back to her rental.

"Evie, darling. Tell me we've bought the farm, so to speak, and you're coming home."

"I'm afraid it's not that simple." She heard his exasperated sigh.

"What the hell is so fascinating in Walker, Texas? You're supposed to get in and get out. What's the holdup?"

"The Richards woman drives a hard bargain."

"Are you thinking with your little brain or your big one at this time?"

"Very funny," said Evie. "Definitely my big one. She told me if we sweetened the deal, she'd be more inclined to sell."

"We've already offered more than it's worth," said Robert. "We're not offering a cent more."

"I want this property. It's prime. It sits on a hill. There's plenty of wind. Buying it for a little more will hardly touch the profits we're going to make."

"What's gotten into you? You're a hard bargain driver."

"She's a tough sell."

"You've bought from tougher, I'm sure."

"Let me crunch some numbers, okay?" said Evie.

"You do what you've got to do. But you need to cut your holiday short. I need you back here."

"I'm not on holiday, Robert." Evie was growing more and more perturbed as the conversation wore on. "I'll work out a new asking price. I'll let you know what it is."

She disconnected the call without waiting for Robert's answer. She wasn't sure why, but his needling really irritated her today. Usually she could take it and give back, but today he simply annoyed her. She felt like he was saying she couldn't do her job. And if there was one thing she knew for sure, she could do her job in her sleep better than anyone else out there.

Evie opened the Richards file. She knew the farm hadn't made money in over six years. She also knew that Beth had debtors right and left. From the feed stores to the stockyards and beyond. Plus there was the second mortgage on the house. That had to scare her, as well.

If Evie paid her what she'd originally offered, Beth would be able to pay off some debts, but that wouldn't leave her with a lot. No wonder she was balking. Beth Richards was anything but stupid.

She came up with the idea to stick with the market value plus some, but sweeten the deal by offering to pay off Beth's debt. There would be no way Beth could refuse that. Feeling very good about things, she closed her laptop and went to Charlie's for a drink.

Evie sat at the bar, drinking a lemon drop martini. She pulled out her phone and googled women's clubs in the area. The search pulled up five strip clubs, a Boys and Girls Club, and a couple of country clubs. Somehow she wasn't surprised. She'd kill for some female contact right about then. Just a little someone to help take the edge off.

"Is this seat taken?" She looked up from her phone to see an older man in a cowboy hat, plaid shirt, and faded jeans barely able to stand. She was trying to figure out how to politely tell him to get lost when Kelsey walked up.

"Evie! So good to see you." To the man, she said, "Excuse me. I'm sitting here."

The man staggered off and Evie thanked her lucky stars Kelsey had shown up when she did. She looked at Beth's younger sister. While Beth's eyes were light, like the sky, Kelsey's were dark like the ocean. She also had long, thick, wavy locks, unlike Beth's short, fine hair.

And personalities? There was no comparison. Kelsey's was outgoing and friendly whereas Beth didn't seem to have one.

"How are you, Kelsey?" said Evie.

"Doing great, thanks. How have you been?"

"I'm hanging in there."

"That's good. I guess?"

Evie laughed.

"It's as good as can be expected at this point in time."

"I heard you had breakfast with my oh-so-pleasant sister today."

"That I did," said Evie. "It was actually quite nice."

Kelsey's eyebrows shot up.

"Is that right? Do tell."

"Well…We didn't kill each other for starters."

"Always a plus," said Kelsey.

"Indeed."

"What did y'all talk about? Or would you rather not say?"

"The usual. I want to buy the farm. She doesn't want to sell. But I think we made headway this morning. I think she's going to think about it."

"Ha! I doubt that. That farm is her life."

"Still. I think we're getting close."

Kelsey grew serious.

"But what will happen to us? To me? To Mama?"

"I'd make sure everyone is taken care of. And wouldn't it be nice to have your own place?"

"But who would take care of Mama?"

"You could pay someone to help take care of her," said Evie. "You could bring in home health care so it wouldn't fall on you and Beth to take care of her all the time."

"But she's *our* mama."

"And she always will be. Y'all could still live together if you want. Or you could put Mama in a memory care place where they specialize in Alzheimer's."

"We're not putting Mama in a home."

"I'm not saying you should. I'm just letting you know you'd have options."

"I don't like those options."

Evie felt her ally in the family pulling away. She took Kelsey's hand.

"Kelsey, all I'm saying is you could get more help for your mom. And that would be a wonderful thing. If you get in-home help, it would be awesome."

"Yeah," said Kelsey. "Extra help would be nice. She doesn't need help showering or anything like that at this point."

"That's great. But just companionship would be nice. It would free you and Beth to follow other pursuits."

"Like what?"

"I don't know. Take a job. Go back to school. The options are practically limitless."

"Yeah. I suppose they are."

"What's wrong, Kelsey? You still seem upset."

"That farm is all we've ever known."

"I understand. But, sometimes, change is a good thing."

"I just need to remember that."

❖

Beth felt like she'd made a deal with the devil. How could she have told Evelyn that she might sell for more money? She couldn't sell the farm. Or could she? Would her grandpappy and pappy understand that she just couldn't do it anymore? Or would they look down on her and see a colossal failure?

Her stomach hurt as she let herself in the house for breakfast. The house smelled delicious and her stomach growled in spite of itself.

"I hope you're hungry," Kelsey said.

"Where's Mama?"

"Still sleeping. How was she last night?"

"Ugh. Restless. And even more confused than usual."

"Have you ever considered getting outside help? From one of those agencies?" said Kelsey.

"And just how would I be able to pay them?"

Kelsey nodded solemnly. "True."

"I'm going to go check on her now," Beth said.

She got to her mama's room and found her sitting on the edge of her bed.

"Good morning," said Beth. "Are you hungry? Kelsey's making pancakes."

"No, thank you. I just ate."

"Mama? You just woke up. You couldn't have eaten."

"Pappy just took me out for a lovely dinner." She smiled.

"I think you were dreaming," Beth offered gently.

"I don't dream." The words came out harshly and the look Mama gave her made Beth want to shrivel up and blow away.

"Okay." She opted to redirect. "Have you used the bathroom yet?"

"I don't know."

"How about we try to go?"

"I don't want to miss Pappy when he comes back to pick me up."

"I wouldn't let that happen," said Beth.

She finally got her mom to the dining room where Kelsey served her a small plate of pancakes and sausage.

"This is delicious," said Mama. "Did the sprites make it?"

"No, Mama." Kelsey laughed. "I did."

Mama squinted at Kelsey.

"You're a liar."

Kelsey looked crestfallen but Beth had to choose her battles.

"Kelsey helped the sprites," said Beth.

"Sprites? What sprites?" said Mama.

Kelsey spun around and left the kitchen. Beth served herself, stomach back in a knot. She didn't know how much more of this either of them could take.

After breakfast, she took Mama out to the porch to enjoy the morning before the ungodly heat arrived.

"Beth?" said Mama.

"What's up?"

"I don't think I'm getting better."

"From what?"

"This brain disease I have."

"Mama," Beth said. "There's no way to get better."

"My brain plays tricks on me all the time. It's hard."

"I can only imagine."

"I think I need to be in a home or something."

"We can take care of you just fine."

"But if I could be around other people like me. I think I'd like that. Think about it, Beth?"

"You got it."

"Not a nursing home, though. I want a place specifically for people with broken brains."

"I understand, Mama. I'll look for one today, okay?" Beth knew they couldn't afford it, but she'd look just to see what was around.

After an hour on the porch, Mama's eyes started to close.

"Come on, Mama. Let's take a nap." She tucked Mama in bed then went out to the kitchen where Kelsey was washing dishes.

"You doing okay?" Beth said.

"Yeah. Sorry. Sometimes it's just so hard."

"I hear you. Look, I've got her lying down so I'm going to head into town. In a moment of lucidity, she asked to be in a place for Alzheimer's patients."

"Do they have those?"

"I'm going to find out. My phone found a couple but I'd like to take a look."

"I wish I could go with you," said Kelsey.

"Me, too. But someone has to stay with her."

"True."

"I'm going to hop in the shower and head out."

"Bring back brochures or something, please."

"Will do."

Beth pulled up in front of the first address she'd found. The building looked like a business building and she was immediately put off. She was about to fire her truck up and put it in reverse when someone tapped on her window. She looked out and saw Evelyn standing there. Fuck. A hard job just got a thousand times harder. She opened her door and got out.

"What are you doing here?"

Evelyn smiled. "It's a small town. I saw your truck and came to say hi. Now I see where you are and thought I'd offer moral support."

"I don't need your support. This is family business. Nothing to concern yourself with."

"Beth, why are you so damned stubborn? You have got to have the biggest chip on your shoulder that I've ever seen. Why be that way?"

Beth was seething. How dare this city slicker talk to her that way.

"Look." She struggled to keep her voice from rising. "All you care about is if I'm selling the farm. Nothing else matters to you. So why do you keep butting in?"

"Maybe I care, Beth. Did that ever occur to you?"

"The only thing you care about is yourself and your damned windmill farm."

"That's not really fair," said Evelyn. "You're presuming an awful lot for not knowing me at all."

"I know you as well as I need to."

"Ouch."

"Whatever. Now, if you'll excuse me, I have to get inside."

"I'm coming with you."

"Why?" Beth just wanted Evelyn to get the fuck away from her, to leave her alone.

"I'm curious."

"You know someone with Alzheimer's?"

"Just your mom."

"You just like to meddle, don't you?" Beth said.

"Why can't you accept that I genuinely care?"

"I know better. You're not coming in. Get lost, Evelyn. Take your genuine caring and stick it up your ass."

"This won't be easy for you. I just thought you'd like some moral support."

"I've got all the moral support I need."

Evelyn looked around.

"Where?"

"Me, myself, and I take care of things day in and day out. This isn't any different. Now, beat it so I can do what I have to do."

"Suit yourself. You'll be sorry."

CHAPTER SIX

Beth watched Evelyn's Mercedes fade from view. She took a deep breath, ran her fingers through her hair, and headed up the walkway. She entered an institutional building. There were doors lining the walls and people in wheelchairs and without in what seemed to serve as a lobby, watching TV and playing games. This wasn't right. Her mama would get lost in a place like that. She turned to leave when someone spoke to her.

"May I help you?"

Beth turned to see a petite woman with long dark hair and kind brown eyes looking at her. She took in the navy blue pencil skirt and jacket and light pink shirt and decided this must be someone in control.

"I, um, I am looking at memory care places. But this doesn't seem right. Sorry to have bothered you."

"You haven't bothered me. And you've barely set foot in the door. You certainly haven't seen our memory care unit."

"Isn't this it?" said Beth.

The woman smiled.

"No. Come on. I'll show you what you came here to see. Then, I'll leave you to be on your way."

Shit. What Beth wanted to see was her mama in her dining room where she belonged. But, as long as she was there…

"Okay. I'll take a look."

"My name's Laura," said the petite woman.

"I'm Beth."

"Nice to meet you. Walk with me, please."

Beth walked through what she knew was a converted hotel. But it seemed overly sanitized. It had no personality. Her mother would be miserable here.

"This is our assisted living area," Laura said. "This is where people with different levels of need live. They all meet in the main room, as you saw."

"Don't they ever leave?"

"All the doors here need a key to open from the inside." Beth nodded her understanding and watched as Laura unlocked a door that led to some gardens. "We often bring the residents out here for fresh air."

Beth took in the paths through the roses and lavender.

"It's really nice out here."

Laura beamed.

"Yes, we all love this area. Who are you looking for a home for?"

"What?"

"You must have someone in mind. Most people don't just decide to look at memory care facilities."

"Right. My mama."

"And she has dementia I take it?" Laura said.

"Alzheimer's."

"I'm so sorry."

"Thanks."

"Well," Laura went on, "you've come to the right place."

Beth stopped staring at the garden. She noticed two houses off to the right down the path.

"Do staff live here?" she said.

"No. Those are our memory care units."

"They're houses."

"Yes, they are," said Laura. "Shall we go look inside?"

Beth's stomach was in knots. Could she really do this to Mama? Put her in a home? Someday she might have no choice. Better have a plan. She shrugged.

"Sure. Let's do this."

Laura let her in a large ranch style house painted in pale yellows and light blues. It was warm and welcoming. Beth liked it despite herself. Laura took her through the kitchen, the library with books and puzzles, and into the activity room where residents were sorting buttons.

"Is there lots for them to do here?" Beth's guilt at just hanging out with her mama most of the time ate at her gut.

"Tons. We have two or three activities a day. They get three meals a day. We help with their meds, ADLs if necessary…"

"What are ADLs?"

"Activities of daily living. Showering, toileting. That sort of thing."

"Mama doesn't need help with those things."

"And that's great. If she's still somewhat independent, she's still welcome here. Now, come on, I'll show you a room."

Beth was duly impressed with the private bedroom. It was spacious enough for a bed and a dresser and she was thrilled that her mama would have a private bath. *If. If* she decided to do this. And that was a big if. But the thought of Mama doing things to keep what was left of her mind sharp, and having care beyond what she and Kelsey could provide made the idea awfully tempting.

"You've been awfully quiet. Would you care to share your thoughts?" Laura said.

"Just kind of taking it all in."

"I understand. Any questions?"

"Yeah. How much does all this cost?"

"Let's go back to my office and we'll talk about that. Does you mom have insurance?"

"Yes. Medicare and a supplement. My dad also left her long-term care insurance."

"Great."

Beth followed Laura to her office and listened to her spiel. She didn't know if she could afford this, but she could take Laura's advice and reach out to Mama's insurance companies.

"Thanks for your time." Beth stood, ready to get back to the farm.

"Here. Take this brochure to look over. My card is in there, so if you have any questions, just reach out, okay?"

"I will."

Beth drove down the road to Catfish Charlie's. She needed a beer. Desperately. Her head was swimming and she still felt guilty over even having gone to that memory care place.

She was sitting at the bar, nursing her second beer when a familiar voice made her skin crawl.

"Is this seat taken?"

She looked up at Evelyn then back to her beer.

"It's a free country," she said.

"Well, I've had warmer invitations, but I'll take it. How was your visit?"

"Good. I guess. I don't know."

"Would you like to talk about it?"

"Why? You only care about your fucking windmills. Not me, not my mama, and probably not even Kelsey."

Evie chose her words carefully.

"You know, Beth. I'm not a monster. I *am* a human being capable of emotions."

"Yeah. Right."

"Fine. I'll go sit somewhere else."

Beth spun on her stool.

"Why did you sit next to me anyway? Why do you continue to bother me? You want the farm, but don't want to pay me what it's worth. You keep showing up trying to ingratiate yourself with me. Like I'm too stupid to know how you are. Give me a break."

That hurt. And Evie couldn't put her finger on why. What did she care what some country bumpkin thought of her and the reasons behind her actions? Yes, she wanted to get her hands on that land. But she also, on some level, for some reason, cared for Beth. The brusque, abrasive woman had gotten under her skin.

She took a moment to examine that. She looked at Beth's profile. Yes, she was an attractive butch woman. And Evie always had had a soft spot for those. But was she interested in her? Really? No. Not that way. She just felt that Beth could use a friend. She doubted she had many.

"How many friends, really good friends, do you have?" said Evie.

"What? Where the hell did that come from?"

Evie shrugged.

"Just curious."

"I get by."

"Maybe I could be your friend."

"I'm not a charity case," sneered Beth. "I don't need you. I do just fine on my own."

"How much time do you spend on social media? How many Facebook friends do you have?"

"Who has time for that?"

"You need an outlet, Beth. Something besides your farm and family."

"I do fine with my life. And don't tell me what I need. You don't know me."

"I'd like to," said Evie. "If you'd just give me a chance."

"Like hell." Beth swallowed the last of her beer. "I should get home."

"One more. I'll buy. Please?"

Beth searched Evie's eyes. Apparently, she saw something there, or maybe it was that she couldn't see anything, so she agreed.

"Two more, Charlie," said Evie. She waited until they'd been served to start the conversation over again. For some reason, she was determined to melt the ice around Beth's heart. One way or another. "Tell me about your childhood, Beth."

"I grew up in Walker. Spent a lot of time on the farm."

Evie laughed.

"Care to expand on any of that?"

Beth shrugged.

"Not much to expand on."

"Who was your best friend in elementary school?" Evie tried again.

"Chuckie Woodsworth."

"Whatever happened to Chuckie?"

"He joined the military right out of high school. He hated Walker. He hated Vernon. He needed to get out. So, he did. Most of the people I went to school with left."

"Why didn't you?"

"I needed to help with the farm," said Beth. "That should be fairly obvious."

Evie ignored the jab.

"What was it like growing up in a small town? I can't imagine."

"What was it like growing up in a big city? You grew up in Dallas, right?"

"Houston. But, yeah, big city."

"It's all you knew, right?" said Beth.

"Sure was."

"That's like Walker. It was all I knew."

"You never dreamed of living anywhere else? Even Vernon?"

"I live on the farm. Or did you forget? I have responsibilities. Which I need to tend to. I've got to go. I'll see you around. Let me know if you ever rework those numbers."

Evie waited until Beth was almost to the door.

"I already have," she called. Beth turned around and stared at her. Evie couldn't read her expression, so she went on. "Let me know when you'd like to get together and discuss them."

Beth checked her watch. Evie held her breath.

"Two hours. Logan's Inn. You're buying."

The light when Beth opened the front door blinded Evie, but she didn't care. She smiled to herself. This was almost a done deal. Charlie was standing in front of her. He let out a low whistle.

"Logan's Inn, eh? That ain't cheap," he said.

"No? What else should I know?"

"People dress fancy to go there. No jeans. No shorts. You'd better go change."

"Then that's what I shall do. Thanks for the tip."

If she had to look nice, Evie wanted to feel nice as well. She took a long, hot shower and dressed in a red cocktail dress with a plunging neckline. She sprayed her Mojave Ghost perfume and walked through it. She looked and smelled amazing. She was ready to make this sale happen.

Evie got to the restaurant with fifteen minutes to spare. She took a table in the bar, ordered a lemon drop, and surveyed the place. It was dark with candles everywhere. The décor, rather than western, had the feeling of an eastern European castle. She felt like she was waiting for Dracula to appear. But she liked the stone walls and the black iron candle holders. She felt comfortable there.

Beth walked in ten minutes late and found Evie in the bar.

"Sorry I'm late." She looked everywhere but at Evie's chest. Evie grinned.

"No, you're not."

Beth was dressed in black slacks with a red, long-sleeved button-down shirt.

"How often do you get to wear that outfit?" Evie said.

Beth shrugged.

"Mostly funerals."

Evie smiled at her.

"Well, you look very nice."

Beth blushed and Evie grew more curious about her. Did she play for Evie's team? Did she have a team? Evie vowed to find out.

"Shall we get a table?" Evie said.

"Sure."

Beth waited for Evie to stand and followed her to the maître d'. Evie thought Beth would make a wonderful butch. She was rude and disrespectful on the outside. But, underneath it all, she had manners and appeared chivalrous. Both traits that made Evie swoon. But she wasn't swooning. Not tonight. This was a business dinner and Evie had long since learned not to mix business with pleasure.

Chapter Seven

"This is a nice restaurant you chose," said Evie.

"Whatever. I figure you can leave on a high note."

"Does this mean you're prepared to accept my offer?"

"No," said Beth. "It means at least you'll have had a good meal when you head back to Dallas."

Evie laughed.

"Is that right?"

"I don't see anything funny about it."

"Oh, Beth. How you underestimate me."

"I think I've made it fairly clear that I'm not selling the farm," said Beth.

"Dinner first. Business after."

"Fine."

"What's good here?" Evie opened her menu.

"What's not? Actually, I get the ribeye."

"Hm. Not really a fan."

The waitress came by and took their order. Evie ordered a bottle of cabernet sauvignon as well.

"I hope that's okay?" she said.

"It's fine. I don't usually drink wine."

"Trust me. This is good stuff."

"If you say so. So, what are we going to talk about since we can't talk business? After all, free dinner and business is the only reason I'm here," Beth said.

"Let's get to know each other."

"Why? You're leaving town in the morning."

"Beth. Look. Let's try to get through the evening, okay? So tell me more about yourself."

Beth shrugged and Evie recognized this as a sign she was uncomfortable.

"What do you want to know?"

"Do you have a boyfriend?" Beth snorted in derision. "A girlfriend?"

"What the fuck?" She lowered her voice. "What do you think I am?"

Evie smiled and held her hands up defensively.

"I don't have any idea who or what you are. That's why I'm asking questions. I gather from your answer that you're homophobic?"

"I'm not afraid of homos."

"That's not what homophobia is, exactly. It means you hate them."

"Hate?" said Beth. "That's a strong word. I don't know any homosexuals, if you must know."

"Yes, you do."

"Who?"

"You know me?"

Beth's eyebrows shot up and she quickly took a sip of wine.

"I'm sorry. I forgot."

"And I'm normal, aren't I?" said Evie.

"You're not normal. You're a pushy, rich, big city girl. Not my idea of normal."

"Oh, Beth. I'm as normal as you. Just a different kind. So, tell me. Do you ever plan on getting married?"

"Who's got that kind of time?"

"What if you didn't have the farm to worry about? Who would you like to date?"

"No one I've met yet. There's not a wide variety of eligible men around here. I don't know where Kelsey finds them all the time."

Evie laughed.

"She does like hookups, doesn't she?"

"That she does. So, what about you? Are you married?"

Beth seemed genuinely curious.

"As you said," said Evie, "who's got time for that?"

"A girlfriend? Anything?"

Evie shook her head.

"Not at this point in time. I'm more of a Kelsey with women, I suppose."

"Really?" Beth looked disgusted. "Doesn't that get old?"

"It does. It really does. I just haven't found Ms. Right yet. Someday."

"I hope so. For your sake."

"That may have been the nicest thing you ever said to me," said Evie.

"Well, if you're into relationships, you deserve to be in a happy one."

"I agree. And I hope someday you find your right person, too."

"Thanks, but I'm more into personal responsibilities."

"Seriously? What do you do for fun, Beth?"

She shrugged again.

"Hang out at Charlie's." A shy smile crept across her lips. "That's pathetic, isn't it?"

Evie put her elbows on the table and rested her chin on her hands.

"Not pathetic. There's just so much more in this big, wide world than Charlie's. Have you ever traveled?"

"Farming is hard work. And I love it. But it's not overly lucrative and you don't exactly get time off to travel."

"No," Evie said. "I don't suppose you do. You should come to Dallas with me."

Beth laughed nervously.

"I don't think I'd know how to act in a big city."

"Just be your normal, charming self. You'd do fine."

Beth laughed a belly laugh then, and something shifted inside Evie. It was a magical sound that she was sure even Beth didn't hear very often. Evie wanted to hear it again.

"Dallas would chew me up and spit me out."

Their dinners arrived and they ate in silence. It was a comfortable silence, though. Evie didn't feel the normal tension radiating from Beth. When the waitress cleared their plates, Evie ordered another bottle of wine.

"That was a really good dinner," said Beth. "Thank you."

"You're welcome. Shall we take our next bottle of wine to the bar to discuss business?"

Beth looked almost disappointed. She quickly recovered.

"Sure. Why not?"

They sat at a table in the far corner, away from the other occupied spots.

"Okay," said Beth. "Hit me with your best shot."

"Are you a Pat Benatar fan?"

"Isn't everyone?" She laughed again and Evie felt herself swooning.

"I need to powder my nose. I'll be right back."

She found the women's room and ran a damp paper towel over her forehead and the back of her neck. She needed to get a grip. She wasn't attracted to Beth. Beth was a mark. A sale. That's all. She needed to get her head on straight. She took a deep breath and went back to the table.

"Welcome back," said a very relaxed Beth. "You ready?"

"Hm?" Evie's mind hit the gutter before she remembered why they were there. "Of course."

She opened her briefcase and pulled out a contract that she hoped Beth would sign.

"What's that?" Beth said.

"It's the contract you need to sign."

"Look, Evelyn—"

"Evie, please."

"Evie…I'm only humoring you. I'm not going to sell."

"I understand, but a girl can dream, can't she?" She set a sheet of paper with numbers on them next to the contract. "Now, here's what I want you to pay close attention to."

Beth crossed her arms over her chest and sat back.

"Fine. Go ahead."

"No," said Evie. "Lean forward and look at them."

Beth did as she was asked.

"There's that just over market value number. I already told you I wasn't interested in that amount."

"Look at these other numbers."

"What are they?"

"Those are your debts."

Beth leaned closer and looked at the long list of debts she'd accumulated. Shit.

"I had no idea…"

"No. And that's okay. Here's the thing. I'm willing to pay you the previously offered amount. And I'll pay off all your debt."

Beth stared at her, not knowing what to say. She finally managed, "You really want my farm, don't you?"

Evie nodded. And smiled.

"Yes, Beth. I really want that farm."

Beth took in the list of debtors and amounts again. It was overwhelming. She'd never be able to pay them all back. Even if she had ten banner years at the farm. Her farm simply didn't produce those kinds of numbers.

"I can't think," said Beth. She stood. "I need to go home and think this over. I don't know. This is too much."

"You can think it over for a day or two. Then I'm going to start taking items away that we're willing to pay. Do you understand?"

"Yeah. I'll see ya."

"Wait."

"What?" Beth just wanted to get out of there. To get away from Evie and her numbers.

"You can't drive. Let's Uber back to the farm."

"I'm fine."

"You're not. Sit down and wait until our ride gets here."

❖

Beth came in for breakfast feeling like she was carrying the weight of the world.

"How was dinner last night?" said Kelsey.

"It was a little overwhelming, to say the least."

"How so?"

"Who did you have dinner with, dear?" asked Mama.

"Someone who wants to buy the farm."

"We're not selling the farm?" There were tears in Mama's eyes.

"I may not have any choice."

"Seriously?" Kelsey's eyes grew wide. "Evie finally got through to you?"

"It's all about the finances. It may be the only way to get out from the debt I've accumulated these past few years."

"We can't sell Pappy's farm," Mama said.

Beth took her hand.

"Don't worry, Mama. We'll take you with us wherever we go."

"I'm not leaving the farm. It's my home."

Beth looked at Kelsey, who said, "Don't worry, Mama. It's all just talk."

"I don't like this kind of talk."

"I'm sorry I upset you," said Beth.

"Don't let me hear you talk like that again. I'm going to take a nap. Y'all sure know how to upset an old woman."

"Shit," Beth said when she heard Mama's bedroom door close.

"Are you honestly thinking of selling?"

"I don't have much of a choice. She wants to give me a chunk of change that would help us all start over and pay off all the farm's debts. I kind of need to do this."

"Oh wow," said Kelsey. "That is awfully tempting. But what about Mama?"

"I don't know. She always asks to go home anyway, so I figure she'll just ask from a different place."

"So did you agree to this? Last night at dinner?"

"I did not. I told her I need to think about it."

"Sounds like your mind's made up. What's going to happen to me, Beth?"

"We'll find a place in Vernon where we can all live together. Or you can get your own place."

"And leave you to deal with Mama alone? I don't think so. Speaking of her, how did those memory care facilities look yesterday?"

"I only checked out one," said Beth. "But it was really nice. I just need to figure out how much insurance will pay to determine if we can afford it."

"But putting her in a home?"

"It's like a big ranch house. And they have activities all day to keep her busy. Better than just sitting around here."

"True. Well, we work puzzles here. And read books…"

"Yes," said Beth. "But for the most part, we sit around the dining room table."

"Yeah. I suppose we do."

"But that might be a moot point. She can stay at the new place with us."

"Have you found a place yet?"

"I haven't looked."

"Just a sec," said Kelsey. She went into the den and got her laptop. She sat next to Beth and fired it up. "Let's start looking. Vernon? Or Walker?"

"Let's check Vernon."

"Fair enough."

Kelsey pulled up a real estate website and they scrolled through the listings.

"Great." Beth was frustrated. "All the nice houses are super expensive."

"Wait." Kelsey stopped scrolling. "What about this one?"

She stopped on a three-bedroom, two-bath house that was selling for an amount that was actually right in their price range. It was painted light gray with white accents and white pillars on the porch.

"That looks nice," said Beth. "Are there pictures of the inside? I bet it's a dump."

The photos of the inside were equally as charming. The bedrooms were a little small, but the kitchen and dining room were spacious.

"I think you'd better go check it out," said Kelsey.

"First I'm going to call Jimmy Smilovic to come appraise the farm and house. I don't want to get ripped off."

"Evie wouldn't rip you off."

"Better safe than sorry."

Jimmy was at their house the following day, which was a good thing, because now that her mind was made up, Beth wanted to get ahold of Evie before she did anything rash.

The appraisal Jimmy gave her was significantly less than what Evie was offering. Significantly.

"Well, that settles it," Beth said. "I'm doing the right thing."

"So go look at that house already," said Kelsey.

"I guess I'd better check in with Evie first."

"House first. Then Evie."

"Okay, okay." Beth dialed the number she'd copied from the listing and scheduled a walk-through for three o'clock that afternoon. She thanked the woman on the other end and hung up.

"Yes!" Kelsey said. "You're making things happen. I'm so proud of you."

"I'm selling out," said Beth. "But I don't have a choice. I'm going to hop in the shower."

"You want me to call Evie for you? Set up a time to meet today?"

"No. Thanks, though. This is my mess so I need to deal with it."

"Don't you have a deadline?"

"I do. And I won't miss it. I need to strike while the iron is hot, as they say. I'm not going to mess this up. I'm going to take care of us. Don't worry about that."

"You always have."

"And I always will."

CHAPTER EIGHT

Beth pulled up to the house on Harrison. It looked as nice as the pictures showed. The yard needed some work, but that wouldn't be an issue.

"Are you Mrs. Richards?" She turned to see a robust woman of around sixty with poorly dyed auburn hair approaching. "I hope I'm not late. I'm Sally Windsor. We spoke on the phone this morning?"

"Right. Nice to meet you. And it's Miss, not Mrs."

"Oh. Right. Well, welcome. Did you want to look inside?"

"Yes. Please."

Sally unlocked the door then stood back and let Beth enter first.

"It's actually quite nice," said Beth. "May I ask why the price is so low?"

"Well, in full disclosure, the last owners were victims of a murder suicide. So it's been quite difficult finding buyers."

Beth nodded as she absorbed that information. No one would need to know this but her. She fell in love with the spacious, airy kitchen and ample dining room. She wandered down the hall to check out the bedrooms. They weren't as small as they looked on the computer, but they weren't roomy either.

She finally walked into the master bedroom, the room where Mama would stay. She studied it closely and decided that all

Mama's furniture would fit. The shower in the master bath would need bars, but Beth could install those. The bathroom wasn't very large, but that was just as well. Mama could get in, do her business and get out.

"So," said Sally. "What do you think?"

"I think I like it. I'd like to buy it."

"Great. Let's go back to my office and fill out the paperwork."

"I actually have another meeting right now. Can we meet tomorrow?"

Sally looked like she didn't quite trust Beth.

"I have others coming to look at the house. I'd really like to lock you in. I'd hate for you to lose it."

"Cancel the others. I'll be at your office at ten tomorrow. We'll go over the paperwork then."

"I'll need to check your credit."

"No, you won't," Beth said.

"What?"

"I'll be paying cash."

Sally looked Beth up and down as if assessing her ability to be able to pay cash for the house.

"May I ask what you do for a living, Miss Richards?"

"I'm a farmer. A very successful one. Trust me. I'll be at your office at ten and we can sign the paperwork."

"Very well. I'll look forward to seeing you tomorrow." But her tone definitely said she doubted Beth would actually show up.

"I'll need the family assessor to come out and look around to make sure it's a good purchase. When can I have him meet you?"

"Have him call me. You obviously have my number."

"That I do." Beth smiled. "I'll have him get in touch with you."

Beth walked down to her car. She sat for a minute before fishing through her pockets for a business card. Not the one Sally gave her. The other one. She finally found it. She flipped it over and saw the cell number written on the back. She sent a text.

Meet me at Charlie's in ten.

She didn't wait for an answer. She drove to Main Street and followed it out to Catfish Charlie's.

"What'll it be?" asked Charlie.

"Bottle of Coors Light, please."

She sat there contemplating the major changes that were about to happen in her life. They were huge and she was anything but a fan of change. She hated it with a passion. But the money. It would be so nice not to be absolutely strapped all the time. That would be very good indeed.

She was lost in thought when the front door opened, letting in painfully blinding sunlight. Beth turned and could barely make out Evie's silhouette against the light. She waved. Evie waved back and walked up to her.

"What do you say we get a booth?" said Evie.

Beth followed her across the room.

"You're not going to have a drink?" Beth said.

"Not until the papers are signed. Then I'll celebrate. Speaking of drinks, how many have you had?"

"Just this one." Beth didn't know what business it was of Evie's.

"Great. Can't sign these papers intoxicated."

"Ah. Got it."

"This is going to take a while," Evie said. "I hope you don't have to be anywhere."

"It won't take that long."

"You know. Just once. You could lose that attitude. Take the edge out of your voice. I'm helping you, Beth. I'm not out to hurt you."

Beth shrugged. She didn't care what Evie thought.

"Can we just do this?" she said.

"No." Evie put the papers back in the briefcase. "Not until you lose the 'tude."

Beth sat back against the booth. Hard. Shit. She needed to make this happen. What did Evie not understand? This was all so Evie could open her damned wind farm.

"Quit acting like you're doing me a favor. This is for you. It's all for you."

Evie clasped her hands in front of her.

"This benefits me, yes. I'm not going to act like it doesn't. But you're getting out from all your debt, plus walking away with a chunk of change. This isn't going to hurt you at all."

What the hell was Beth's problem? Just this morning she'd resigned to do this. Then she saw the house, met with the Realtor. She'd even been excited. But now, she wanted to rip up Evie's papers and wipe that smug look off her face. She took a deep breath. This had to happen. The sooner, the better.

"Okay. You're right." She exhaled. "Let's go ahead and do this."

Evie stared at her.

"I'm serious." Beth fought to keep any edge out of her voice. "I want to do this."

"Great." Evie beamed. "Let's do this indeed."

Evie was realizing just how much she'd miss this country bumpkin with the chip on her shoulder. Beth had grown on her. Like a fungus, she supposed.

She opened her briefcase and pulled out some papers.

"It's really too dark here to do this. Let's head to my rental and sign these there."

Beth looked at her as if assessing her motives. She must not have detected anything weird because she agreed and stood.

Evie blinked in the bright sunlight.

"Shall I drive?"

"I'll follow you," said Beth.

"Suit yourself."

It was a five-minute drive to her Airbnb. Beth parked behind her on the driveway and they walked in together.

"You look very nice, by the way." Evie took in Beth's navy golf shirt and long khaki cargo shorts.

"Thanks. I had an appointment before I went to Charlie's."

"A good appointment?"

"Yeah," Beth answered enthusiastically. "A really good appointment."

"Great. Okay. Let's sit in the dining room. It's nice and airy and well lit."

"Yeah. This is much easier on the eyes than Charlie's."

Evie laughed.

"No doubt. Now, let's get to it." She took out a sheet of paper. "This is your list of outstanding debts."

Beth stared at them.

"All of this? I owe all of this?"

"Not after you sign the papers." Evie smiled. Beth looked like she might puke. "Are you okay?"

Beth nodded.

"Shit. I didn't realize how badly I'd fucked up."

"Don't think like that. You did the best you could to keep the farm afloat. Now, I need you to study this list hard, Beth. I need to know if there's anything we missed. I'll add it now. Once we've signed the papers, it's a done deal."

Beth studied the list, leaving Evie with nothing to do but watch her. She thought again what a fine butch Beth would be. If she went that way. Sure, she'd never been around lesbians before, but if she realized they existed, would she feel compelled to join the tribe?

"Charlie's?" Beth said.

"What about it?"

"My tab for Charlie's is on here."

"Any outstanding debt, Beth. Any and all. We're taking care of them."

Beth nodded slowly.

"Obviously. This is quite an extensive list."

"Did we miss anything?"

"I don't think so."

"Great. Go ahead and sign and date."

The rest of the paperwork went smoothly. Soon everything was signed and dated. Beth sat ramrod straight as if waiting to sign more. Evie leaned back against her chair.

"So that's it," Evie said. "It's done."

"So it is. How long do I have to get out of the house?"

"I'll give you time. Not like six months or anything, but some. How much time do you think you'll need?"

"When will I get the money?"

"I haven't worked that out yet."

"I need it by ten tomorrow."

"Morning?!" said Evie.

"Yeah."

"Are you serious?"

"Yeah."

Evie stared into Beth's pale blue eyes. Belying the bravado of her voice, her eyes showed fear and worry.

"Okay then. Let me get that wired. Excuse me for one moment."

Evie stepped into the spare room which had served as an office for her. She dialed Robert's number.

"Tell me it's a done deal finally," Robert answered.

"It is. I need you to wire the money to Beth's bank tonight."

"What? After all the time she made us wait? Suddenly it's gotta be expedited? I don't think so."

"Robert, please. For me?"

"Ugh. It's important to you?"

"Yes."

"Have you slept with her yet?"

"No." But Evie laughed. "I'm the first lesbian she's ever met."

"Oh, honey. Don't get your heart broken."

"I don't have a heart, remember?" Evie said.

"I'll wire the money now."

"Thanks. See you soon."

Beth was slumped back against her chair when Evie walked in.

"Done deal. It's happening right now," Evie told her.

"Great. Thanks."

"Do you mind telling me why you need the money so soon?"

"If you must know, I'm buying a house."

"Already? Beth, this is awfully quick. You need to wait some time. Make sure it's what you want. Has Kelsey seen it?"

"Kelsey wants me to buy it. I wouldn't do this without her being onboard."

"And the Realtor is okay with this quick sale?"

"Yeah," said Beth. "She really wants to get the house off her hands."

"How about some champagne? To celebrate?"

"I don't really like champagne. Do you have beer?"

"When was the last time you had champagne?"

Beth shrugged.

"When I was a kid. At my cousin's wedding. It was gross."

"Okay. Well, the champagne I have is very expensive and very good. Please say you'll join me for a glass."

"Whatever."

Evie laughed.

"I'll take that as a yes."

She filled two flutes and handed one to Beth.

"To new beginnings," she said.

"Indeed."

She watched Beth take an apprehensive sip. Then she saw her eyes grow wide with surprise.

"This is really good," said Beth.

"I told you you'd like it. Now, stand up. This celebration needs a hug."

Beth stood and walked over to Evie. Evie wrapped her arms around Beth's neck and Beth finally wrapped hers around Evie's waist. Something shifted inside Evie. Something she'd been fighting the whole time she'd been in that Podunk town. Her heart fluttered hard against her chest. Fearing Beth might feel it, she regretfully stepped back.

Sure her face was flushed, Evie immediately turned away and walked to the refrigerator.

"I bought some finger food, too," she called over her shoulder. "Are you hungry?"

"Sure."

Evie took a deep breath and brought the tray of meats and cheese and bread to the table. She hoped the refrigerator had cooled the heat in her face.

Beth helped herself to the tray.

"You thought of everything, didn't you?"

"Mm. This deal calls for a celebration. And I do know how to celebrate."

"Beats the hell out of celebrating at Charlie's."

"No doubt. And here's the thing, Beth. There's no set end to this celebration. So relax and enjoy yourself."

"I think I will."

"Do you like to dance, Beth?"

"Not particularly."

"When was the last time you danced? At your cousin's wedding?"

Beth laughed, a magical sound.

"Something like that."

"What kind of music do you like?" Evie said.

"Merle Haggard, Waylon Jennings, Hank Jr."

Evie groaned inwardly.

"Okay. You're going to learn new music today. And we're going to dance, and drink champagne and party down."

Beth laughed again.

"If you say so."

Evie pulled up her music app and searched for dance hits of the nineties. The first song was “Believe” by Cher. Evie stepped into the living room where the Bluetooth speakers were and moved and grooved to one of her all-time favorite songs.

She glanced over at Beth who had a crooked grin on her face. Evie danced toward her. She took Beth’s hand and gave it a tug.

“Dancc with mc?”

CHAPTER NINE

Beth looked at Evie's outstretched hand. She almost wanted to take it. She almost wanted to dance with her. But she didn't want to make a fool of herself.

"I don't know how to dance to this kind of music."

"How can you not know how? You just move to the music. Come on. I'll help you."

Evie's smile, her excitement, everything about her was contagious. Beth took her hand and stood. Evie didn't let go of her hand as they made their way to the living room. And Beth found herself hanging on to Evie's hand like a lifeline.

The song had ended by the time they were ready to dance.

"Bummer." Beth laughed and sat on the couch.

"Oh no you don't. I'll restart it. Now come on."

The song started again and Evie was moving her hips seductively as she stood in front of Beth, arms extended. Beth didn't take Evie's hands. She stood though and found herself within millimeters of Evie. She got a whiff of Evie's subtle perfume. She smelled good. How had Beth not noticed that before?

"You okay?" said Evie.

"Huh? Yeah. Fine. Now, show me how to dance, please."

"Just move to the rhythm. Start by swaying your hips." Evie placed her hands on Beth's hips and tried to make them move. Something short-circuited in Beth's brain. She couldn't breathe.

She couldn't move. Something was wrong with her. She sat back down on the couch.

"Are you all right?" Evie sat next to her.

"I don't know. Something's wrong. Give me a minute to catch my breath."

"I'm worried about you. Maybe you've had too much champagne. Let me get you a glass of water."

"Thanks."

As soon as Evie left the room, Beth began feeling better. She could breathe again. Her head didn't feel full of cotton, and the blood rushing in her ears had subsided.

"Here's some water. Just sip it, okay?"

Beth gratefully took a sip of the cold fluid. It felt good in her fevered body.

"Sorry," Beth said. "I don't mean to be a killjoy. We can try again in a few."

"Only if you're okay. Tell me. What happened?"

"I don't know. I was fine and then I couldn't breathe. I got hot all over. I could feel my blood pulsing in my ears." She looked over and saw Evie smiling. "You think this is funny?"

"No, Beth. It's not. I just don't think it's anything serious."

"Neither do I. As soon as you went to get the water, I started feeling better."

"Listen, I know you've never kissed anyone before."

"What the hell does that have to do with anything?" Beth was losing her temper.

"Have you ever had a crush on anyone?" Beth shook her head. "Do you like me, Beth?"

"I don't dislike you as much as I used to."

Evie laughed.

"Well, that's a start anyway." Beth stared at her, obviously confused. "I think you should go home, Beth."

"But I want to hang out. I want to learn to dance. I'm not ready to go home."

"Are you absolutely sure?"

"Yeah."

"Okay," said Evie. "This time I'll give you some space so you can see if you can feel the rhythm on your own."

Beth was disappointed, but she wasn't sure why. She stood, Evie restarted the song, and Beth watched Evie watching her.

"Are you going to dance? Or are you going to stare at me?"

"I'll dance." Evie started moving around the living room, as if possessed by some gentle spirit. Beth moved her hips but felt ridiculous. She moved her arms and feet and soon was enjoying herself immensely as one upbeat song after another flowed through the speakers.

She didn't twist and turn and move around as much as Evie did, but watching Evie made her happy. Soon they were both laughing and dancing, and Beth couldn't remember the last time she'd had this much fun.

A slow song came on and Beth found herself feeling faint again. Her head got foggy and her heart raced. The blood pulsed in her ears. What the hell was wrong with her?

"Time for a champagne break," Evie announced. Beth followed her to the dining room. "You okay? You look a little peaked."

"I'm fine," Beth lied. "Just ready for more champagne."

"I hope you don't mind that I turned off the music. I just wasn't sure you were ready to slow dance with me."

"With you?"

"Well, there's no one else here is there?" She laughed.

"No," said Beth. "I don't suppose there is. That's fine that you turned the music off. I don't know how to slow dance anyway."

"I'd be happy to teach you." Evie knew she was pushing the envelope, but now that she'd made her buy, her new goal was to get Beth to bed. She wanted her. There was no denying that. And she believed in her heart of hearts that Beth wanted her, too. Evie just needed to make sure Beth figured it out on her own, which could prove tricky indeed.

"Maybe next time a slow song comes on," said Beth.

"Sounds good." Evie smiled her best smile at Beth. It was a smile that had served her well throughout her life. Beth grinned then looked away. This was going to be most difficult.

Beth's phone pinged. Evie resented the intrusion, but sat quietly as Beth read and responded.

"Anything important?" said Evie.

"Kelsey. Just wants to know when I'll be home."

"Is your mom okay?"

"I assume so. Kelsey just wants to go to town. I suppose I should get home so she can."

Evie felt like someone had poured a bucket of ice on her.

"Not yet. We're still dancing."

"Sorry." Beth stood. "I've got to go."

"I'll swing by your place on my way out of town tomorrow. To give you your copies of the forms you signed."

"I won't be home."

"Then swing by here when you're finished with your business. I'll wait for you."

"You sure? I don't know how long it'll take."

"One more day in Vernon won't hurt," said Evie.

"Great." Beth positively beamed. Evie grinned to herself. Progress was being made.

"May I ask one favor before you go?" said Evie.

"What's that?"

"May I have a hug?"

Beth looked a little self-conscious, then shrugged.

"Sure. Why not?"

Evie stepped into Beth's arms, her strong, muscular arms, and swooned at Beth's tight stomach. Every inch of Evie was alive with need. She could feel Beth trembling and fought to maintain control, to not take Beth's hand and lead her to the bedroom. Oh, Evie had such plans for Beth. But Beth wasn't ready. Would she ever be?

After Beth left, Evie sat at the dining room table smiling to herself. She already had Beth's paperwork for her. She told her she didn't for one reason and one reason only. She wanted, no *needed*, to see Beth again.

She put the glasses in the dishwasher and tossed the empty champagne bottle. Her body hummed with unspent passion. She needed to get out. She needed to expend some of the pent-up energy. She headed for Charlie's.

There was a decent crowd there for a weeknight, so Evie ordered her lemon drop martini and took it to a booth. A cowboy soon sat down across from her.

"You're looking mighty lonely," he said.

"Au contraire. I'm anything but lonely."

"Well, I can't have a beautiful lady like yourself sitting alone. Would you like to dance?"

Evie tried not to tell the cowboy to fuck off. Besides, the twang coming out of the jukebox was not dancing music.

"No, thank you." She tried to smile sweetly. "I'm actually waiting for someone."

"Who's the lucky fella?"

"Hey, Evie, sorry I'm late." Kelsey walked up just in time.

"Heya, Kelsey," said the cowboy.

"Hey, Rich. Will you excuse us?"

"Sure thing."

"Your timing is impeccable," Evie whispered. "Next one's on me."

"Not necessary. Happy to help. It's about time for Rich to get home to his wife anyway."

"Is that right?"

"Mm-hm."

"Loser," said Evie.

"I'll drink to that." They clinked glasses. "What are you doing here? I thought you'd be packing."

"There'll be time for that. Besides, Beth needs to come by my place tomorrow to pick up her papers."

Kelsey nodded.

"Did she tell you we're buying a house?"

"She did."

"She was at your place long enough. What the hell were you doing? I thought y'all were talking business."

"We were." Evie fought not to blush.

"She's pretty damned excited about it. I guess she's actually paying for it and signing papers tomorrow."

"That's great," Evie tried to sound enthusiastic. "Fantastic, even."

"Yeah. She went and looked at it today and is paying cash for it in the morning. That's all I got out of her. She was in a foul mood when she got home."

"I wonder why," said Evie. "She was fine when she left my place."

"She's always in a foul mood. Beats me. I think she needs to get laid, personally."

Evie laughed out loud.

"That does seem like the answer to all of life's woes, does it not?"

"Hear, hear. I'll drink to that."

Evie wanted to grill Kelsey and find out all Beth's secrets. How far could she push without being obvious?

"I can't believe she's never had a boyfriend."

"Or a girlfriend." Evie arched her eyebrows. "Oh, come on. She's like a classic butch dyke."

"You think?"

"I do. I wish she'd realize it so she could find happiness." Kelsey took a sip of her drink. "I really would like to see her happy before I die."

"Yes. Happiness is a good thing. What about you?" said Evie. "Don't you deserve to be happy?"

"I suppose. It's going to take getting out of this nowhere town for that to happen."

"Where will you go? And when? You don't want to waste your whole life waiting for the right time."

"Those are all good questions. I'm here for the duration for Mama, though. She's our first priority."

"What if you put her in a care home? Or hire caregivers? Then you'd be free to do as you please."

"Who knows?" said Kelsey. "Maybe someday I'll show up on your doorstep."

"Both you and your sister are welcome any time."

"Right. Like Beth would ever leave this Podunk town. She's married to it, I swear."

"You may be right. I wish her much happiness, though. Wherever she ends up."

"Here's to happiness," said Kelsey as she raised her glass. She finished her drink.

"I'm buying this round." Evie made her way to the bar and was soon back with two drinks. "Do you dance?"

"Of course. Shall we?"

"Does the jukebox play anything but honky-tonk?"

"Not really."

"Is there another bar in town?"

"Woody's. But it's a biker bar."

"That's not my style either. Surely there's someplace we can dance."

"We can head back to the farmhouse. If Mama's in bed, we can dance in the living room. Come on, Ev. Say you'll go? I'm in the mood to partay."

"What about Beth?" said Evie.

"Maybe we can get her to dance, too. Though I wouldn't hold my breath."

"You never know, Kelsey. You just never know."

CHAPTER TEN

Beth felt lousy. Something was off and she couldn't pinpoint what. She didn't feel feverish anymore. More like empty. She felt like something was missing.

She'd read to Mama, who had been very agitated and insisted Beth was reading the story all wrong. She finally announced she was going to bed and Beth heard all her routine getting ready for bed sounds. Then there was silence. She peaked in at Mama and she was lying there with her eyes closed. Beth breathed a sigh of relief.

But now she was restless. She wanted to do something but couldn't figure out what. Her mind drifted back to dancing with Evie and she thought that was exactly what she wanted to be doing. But she couldn't. So why couldn't she just let it go?

She sat at the dining room table with a glass of sweet tea and thought about tomorrow. She'd be a homeowner. Like, of a house she bought herself. She was feeling better and very proud of herself when her phone buzzed.

She checked her watch. It was nine o'clock. Who would be texting at that hour?

On our way home.

It was from Kelsey. Odd that she would be coming home so early.

Who's with you?

Evie.

Beth smiled. This made her happy. Why? She didn't know, but she knew her night had just gotten loads better.

She quickly dried the dinner dishes and put them away. She looked around. The house looked good. She wouldn't be embarrassed. She poured herself two fingers of tequila, sat in the easy chair in the family room, and waited.

The front door opened a little while later and in walked Kelsey and Evie. Kelsey positively shone while Evie looked more apprehensive. Beth wondered what they were up to.

"Y'all are home early," said Beth.

"We want to dance. Dance with us, Beth?" Kelsey said.

"Dance? You two?"

Evie nodded and Kelsey said, "Did I stutter?"

Beth didn't like the idea of Evie and Kelsey dancing together. In fact, it pissed her right off. Why? Who knew? Who cared? She wanted to be an asshole and storm out of the room, but Evie's next words stopped her.

"We came here because I wanted to dance with you. I hope that's okay?"

Beth shrugged.

"Sounds good."

"I'll go make drinks," Kelsey said.

"I've got one." Beth held up her glass. Kelsey gave her a thumbs-up as she went to the kitchen.

Evie crossed the room to where Beth sat.

"I hope you don't mind. I just really had a good time with you earlier. But, if I'm intruding, please say so."

Beth felt herself grow calmer, less tense. She even managed a smile.

"You're not intruding. Not in the least. This should be fun."

"You know something? You've got a great smile. You really should smile more often."

Beth felt the heat creeping over her face. She thought it odd, since she'd only just started her drink. But that must be it, right?

"I'll try to remember that," she said.

Kelsey was back with drinks and Beth felt conflicted. On one hand, she felt like Kelsey had intruded. On the other, she found that she could breathe again. Her chest had been feeling tight and she was starting to grow concerned that maybe something was wrong. But she was feeling fine now, so she pushed it out of her mind.

"Let's turn on some tunes," Kelsey said.

"Not too loud. Mama's asleep," said Beth.

Kelsey closed the pocket doors to the hall.

"Problem solved." She turned to Evie. "What sort of music have you got?"

"Every kind. I'm in a disco kind of mood, though."

"Disco?" Beth scrunched up her face. "Seriously?"

"Sure. The Bee Gees. Donna Summer. Smooth, sensuous, and with a beat that anyone can dance to."

"Almost anyone," Beth said.

Evie laughed and set her phone down.

"Do y'all have Bluetooth speakers?" she asked.

"We're not really high-tech," said Kelsey.

"Gotcha. Okay. My phone will work just fine on its own."

Beth listened to the music as Evie stared at her.

"This isn't bad. What are we listening to?"

"Soundtrack from *Saturday Night Fever*. Only the epitome of disco." Kelsey started dancing and Evie held her hand out to Beth. "Join us?"

"Maybe next song."

"Suit yourself," said Kelsey. "We're going to dance the night away."

After the first song, a slow song came on. Evie was back at Beth's chair.

"Please?" she said.

"Fine." Beth stood and cast a glance at Kelsey who was moving in a circle with her eyes closed.

"Do you want to dance with me? Or alone?" said Evie.

Beth shrugged.

"I'll dance with you."

She stood in front of Evie, focused on the floor.

"Look at me," Evie said. Beth raised her chin. "Now, put your hands on my waist."

Beth did as she was instructed. Evie placed her hands on Beth's shoulders.

"Now guide me around."

Beth looked back to her feet and slowly but surely started moving with the music.

"Must you always look down?" Evie laughed.

Beth looked up again, but Evie was staring at her. And when their gazes met, Beth found it hard to breathe. Her body was humming again and she was starting to suspect it had something to do with Evie. Which struck her as odd.

"Look at you two go," said Kelsey. "Y'all make a cute couple."

Beth blushed furiously and turned to make a comment.

"Eyes on me," Evie said.

Beth turned back to her as the song ended.

"There's nothing wrong with being cute," Evie whispered. "It's not a bad thing."

The next song was still somewhat slow, but not hold each other slow.

"'Night Fever,'" said Evie. "One of my all-time favorites. Come on. Both of you."

They came together in a group and danced. Beth felt weird dancing with her sister, but at least she could breathe. They danced to song after song and Beth was having a fantastic time.

The flush on Beth, along with the smile, looked good on her. She was indeed a fine looking butch and Evie wished she could figure out a way to let her know what she was. She'd have to come to her own conclusions, but damn, Evie wanted to help her get there. In so many ways.

The old grandfather clock chimed one and Beth sat down.

"What gives?" Evie said.

"I'm going to finish my drink and head to bed. I've got an appointment in the morning and I can't drag myself in there dog-tired. It's been fun though. You all carry on."

"No." Evie didn't want to dance if Beth wasn't going to. "You're right. It's late. And I've got those papers to get ready for you."

"Oh yeah." Beth seemed to brighten. "Can't forget that."

"No way." Evie flashed her best smile. "I look forward to seeing you tomorrow."

"Me, too." Beth finished her drink. "Good night, you two."

"Good night," Evie said. She looked at Kelsey. "You okay with calling it a night?"

"I suppose so. This was fun. We should do it again." Evie laughed. "What?"

"I'm leaving tomorrow. Going back to Dallas."

"Oh yeah. Lucky."

Evie smiled at Kelsey.

"You'll get there. Some day."

"God, I hope."

Evie was careful driving home. She'd only had two drinks at Beth's, but she'd been steadily drinking all day. She didn't need any trouble.

She got home without incident and went to bed. She tossed and turned, but couldn't sleep. She finally got up, ran a hot bath, and willed herself to relax. She finally climbed back into bed and fell fast asleep.

Morning came too early, but with it came the promise of seeing Beth again. Beth. The surly, crabby, defensive irritant had turned into so much more. So very much more. Evie really liked her. Too bad she was clueless.

No worries. Evie would soon be back in Dallas, enjoying all the women it had to offer. Beth would soon no longer even be a blip on Evie's radar. The thought made her sad. Damn, maybe Robert was right. Maybe Beth had gotten to her more than she cared to admit.

Over coffee, she got Beth's paperwork in another folder, wrote her name on the tab, and settled in to wait. She was getting hungry and was about to leave to get some food when her phone buzzed. It was Beth.

On my way. Is this a good time?

Great. I'll be waiting.

Evie went into the bathroom and scrubbed away the coffee breath. She then popped an Altoid just to be safe. She was ready. It was time to say good-bye.

She watched Beth pull into the driveway and stepped out to greet her. Without thinking, she hugged Beth close. To her surprise, Beth hugged her back.

"What was that for?" Beth asked when Evie stepped away.

"I don't know. I just felt like it. Hope it was okay?"

"Sure. It was fine."

"Come on in," said Evie. "I've got your paperwork all ready."

"Great." Beth exhaled. "Just what I need. More paperwork."

"That reminds me. How'd your meeting go?"

"Great." She fished a key out of her pocket. "I'm the proud new owner of a house."

"I want to see it."

"Do you? Do you have time? Because I'd love to show you."

"I know," said Evie. "Let's get some food and have a picnic."

"Sure thing. You want to drive? Or should I?"

"I'll drive. My car is much more comfortable, I'm sure."

They drove through a fried chicken stand then Evie let Beth give her directions to her new home. Her excitement was contagious and Evie couldn't wait to see the place. They crossed over Willbarger and Evie could feel the neighborhoods change. She drove past some pretty sketchy places.

Finally, she pulled up in front of an adorable house.

"This is it," Beth said. "Isn't it awesome?"

"It really is. I'm so happy for you."

"Come on. I'll show you inside."

Beth grabbed the bag of food and Evie grabbed her free hand. When Beth squeezed her hand, Evie decided not to let go.

"I need my key." Beth held up their joined hands. Evie reluctantly let go.

Beth opened the door then stood back to let Evie enter. It was a nice sized place. And Evie followed Beth, who gave her the grand tour.

"Nice master," said Evie. "Is this yours?"

"No. It's where Mama will sleep. It will be more familiar to her, you know?"

"True. That's very thoughtful of you, Beth."

Beth shrugged.

"It's the least I can do for her."

"When are you moving in?"

"Soon. At least I hope soon. I've got to get boxes and probably a U-Haul for a day or two. I want to make it as smooth and painless for Mama as possible. Don't want to drag it out by having boxes all over the house for days on end."

Evie nodded her understanding.

"You know something?"

"What's that?"

"For someone who tries to come off as a hard-ass, you are a very caring individual," Evie said.

Beth shrugged again. Evie hadn't meant to make her uncomfortable, but she had to call it how she saw it.

"If I care about someone, I don't mind showing it."

"Do you care about me?"

"Sure. I never thought I would though." Beth laughed.

"Let's eat. I'm famished."

Evie wanted to push the envelope. She was dying to get Beth to admit she had feelings for her. Baby steps. She knew she'd have to take baby steps. Only she didn't have time for that. Ugh. It would have to be a compromise. She'd push a little harder after lunch. She had plans that included Beth and she didn't want to leave town until those plans had been realized.

CHAPTER ELEVEN

Beth felt like her chest would explode. She was so proud and she derived such great pleasure from sharing her new home with Evie, who seemed duly impressed. She was enjoying her chicken strips and loving the company when it hit her that after this, she'd never see Evie again. The thought made her sad.

"Can I ask you a personal question?" she said.

"Sure. I'm an open book."

"No. Not that kind of question. It's just…that is…I was wondering…"

"Spit it out." Evie laughed. "What's on your mind?"

"Can we keep in touch?" There. She'd blurted what was on her mind. She held her breath waiting for a reply.

"I'd like that, Beth. I'd like that very much."

"Yeah?"

"Yeah. We can text, email, call, whatever works for you."

"That would be awesome."

"I agree," said Evie. "Let me have your phone."

"Why?"

"So I can enter my info in your contacts, silly."

"Ah," said Beth. "But I already have your number."

"Then I'll enter my email address. In case you decide to email me sometime."

She handed her phone to Evie and her heart raced as she watched Evie enter her information. She didn't know how smart this would be, but she had to do it. For some reason, she couldn't let Evie just ride off into the sunset.

On one hand, Evie felt dangerous. She had an effect on Beth that she couldn't explain. On the other, she knew she'd miss Evie more than she should. Why? She couldn't answer that.

Evie handed Beth her phone and their fingers touched. Beth felt like she'd placed her fingers in an outlet. She dropped the phone.

"You okay?" Evie said.

"Fine. I think."

They were sitting on the floor in the living room, backs against the wall. Beth was full and content. Evie scooted over a few inches until their shoulders touched. Sparks flew again and Beth thought about it. Sparks? Sparks flying? She'd read about things like that. She wondered. No, it couldn't be possible. Not Evie.

"You okay?" Evie said again.

"Fine."

"You just stiffened up like a flippin' board. You want me to move away? Am I too close?"

Beth thought for a minute before responding.

"Nah. You're fine."

Evie took Beth's hand in hers.

"I like you, Beth. Like *really* like you."

Her words were like a punch in the gut. Beth didn't know how to respond. She only knew Evie made her heart race and confused the hell out of her.

"I like you, too."

"Talk to me, Beth. There's something going on in that brain of yours."

"Not really."

"Really," said Evie. "Be open with me. Tell me what you're thinking."

I'm scared. I like you so fucking much and it terrifies the hell out of me.

Beth shrugged.

"I don't know. You make me feel things. Things I don't understand."

"Like what?"

"Look. I'm just confused. That's all," said Beth.

"I can help with that." Evie's voice was soft, inviting.

"You think so, huh?"

"Beth, look at me."

Beth turned her head and gazed into the most beautiful pools of chocolate she'd ever seen. How had she never noticed Evie's eyes before? Her gaze dropped to her full lips, coated with a light pink lipstick. Her pulse raised. Her heart was galloping, and Beth feared it would come out of her chest.

"See?" Evie said. "I'm not so scary. Now, let's talk about your confusion."

Beth looked away again.

"I don't know if I can."

"Look at me. Don't look away." Beth exhaled heavily but looked back at Evie. "You like me, right? But you get confused because I scare you. You don't understand your body's reaction to me."

Beth swallowed hard.

"Something like that." Her voice cracked. But Evie didn't seem to notice. Her gaze was boring into Beth and it took every ounce of strength not to look away.

"I'm going to do something now Beth. Something we both want."

"What's that?"

"I need your permission though. I do hope you'll say yes."

"What is it? You're scaring me."

"Beth? May I kiss you?"

Don't look away. Don't look away. Can she kiss me? Is that what I want? What can it hurt?

Beth nodded slightly. It was all she could manage. She watched Evie looking at her lips and her heart took off again. When Evie closed her eyes and leaned in, Beth forced herself not to pull away. Instead, she closed her eyes and waited.

Evie's lips were soft, tender, and featherlight. The kiss lasted only a second and left Beth wanting more. Her blood was pounding in her ears again and she worried she'd have a heart attack from the fluttering in her chest. Her whole body was on fire and she felt like a pile of mush. Was this supposed to happen? One kiss?

"Well?" said Evie softly.

"May I have another?"

"Beth, my dear, you may kiss me anytime you want."

Beth kissed Evie then. She didn't have a clue what she was doing, but she kissed her hard over and over, her lips pulling on Evie's, needing each kiss. And so much more. But what? What more did she want? The question scared her.

Beth pulled away, breathless. She was dizzier than she'd ever been in her life and she had electrical currents coursing through her veins. She leaned in and kissed Evie again.

Oh, damn. Evie had it bad. And Beth was a natural. Knowing she'd never been kissed before, Evie was prepared for wet, sloppy kisses. But Beth's were anything but. They were forceful, demanding, and so fucking arousing.

Evie focused on keeping her hands to herself, but with each kiss, it was clear she was fighting a losing battle. She ran her hand up and down Beth's arm then moved it to her leg. When she placed her hand on Beth's sculpted thigh, she almost climaxed on the spot.

Beth leaned harder into Evie and Evie slid back onto the floor. Beth was on top of her, kissing her, making her crazy. Evie slid her tongue out against Beth's lips. Beth hesitated a second before opening her mouth and letting Evie in.

Beth's tongue made frantic laps around Evie's mouth. She stroked Evie's tongue with her own and moaned into Evie's mouth. Evie was in heaven.

Evie finally broke the kisses and got herself into a sitting position.

"What?" Beth looked up at her from the floor.

"We need to stop. Or we'll end up doing something you're not ready for."

"What? I'm ready. I'll do anything. Just please let me kiss you again."

Damn, she was hot. And looking at Beth with her flushed skin, heavy eyelids and glistening eyes, Evie had to use every ounce of self-control not to peel Beth's jeans off, climb out of her own clothes, and press Beth's face between her legs. But now wasn't the time.

"Come on, babe. Sit up."

"Babe?"

"Is that okay?"

"Sure," said Beth. She grinned. "I like it."

"Good. Because I want you to be my babe."

"And what shall I call you?"

"Whatever you like, babe. Anything at all."

"So are you my girlfriend?" said Beth.

Girlfriend. That entailed commitment. Something Evie was dead-set against. She pondered only briefly before replying, "I guess I am."

"Right on."

Evie would love to see where this…whatever it was…would take her. She liked Beth. Could she be true to her? Something inside made her feel like she could. Her feelings about Beth were different. Very different from what she was used to.

Evie's phone rang. Shit. It was Robert.

"Give me just a sec, okay?"

"Sure."

"Robert. What's up?"

"Are you on your way home from Podunk?"

"Not quite. I'll be home soon. Just don't know when," said Evie.

"What the hell? You bought the property. We sent the Richards woman her money. I need you here. I need you to help run the place."

"I know. I know, but give me another day or two, okay?"

"Did you get her in bed?"

"Robert!"

"What? You did, didn't you? So now's the time for you to make your world famous escape."

"It's not like that," Evie said.

"What is it then? What the hell is keeping you there?"

"Look, I'll be home soon. I'll call you when I leave." She hung up.

"That's right. You've got to go home, don't you?" said Beth.

"I'm afraid so."

"Shit. What the fuck am I doing?"

"Sh. Come here." She pulled Beth to her chest and ran her fingers through Beth's hair. "We'll work something out. I promise. You could come to Dallas with me."

"And who would take care of Kelsey and Mama?"

"I think it's time for Kelsey to take care of Kelsey. And you can place your mom."

Beth sat up.

"If only it was that easy."

"Yeah. I know. But I meant what I told Robert. I'm not going to leave for a few days. So we'll have time to explore this thing between us."

"I hope so."

"I promise, babe. Now, come on. Let's get our mess cleaned up and make plans for getting you moved."

"Good idea. Although my head's so fuzzy, I don't think I'll ever be able to think clearly again." Beth laughed.

"I'm here to help. In any way I can."

"I do appreciate that."

"I have an idea. Let's go out to your place. We can pick up your mom and go for an outing. Then tomorrow, I'll take her by myself so you can pack and do everything you need to."

"That would be great," Beth said. "Though there's no guarantee she'll go anywhere with you."

"But if she goes with me today…"

"There's no guarantee she'll remember you tomorrow, sweetheart."

Evie tried to focus on what Beth was saying, but she was swooning at the term of endearment.

"I get that," she finally said. "But it's worth a try, isn't it?"

"It sure is."

"Okay. I'll follow you out there and then we'll go out in my car. Where's a good place to go?"

"Mama loves feeding the ducks on the lake. We keep a bag of birdseed just for that."

"Great. We'll do that."

They arrived at the farmhouse and found Kelsey sitting at the dining room table with her head down.

"What's up?" said Beth. "Look who I brought home."

Kelsey looked up. "Hey."

"What's wrong?" said Evie.

"It's just been a really long day. She's in a bad space and nothing I could do soothed her."

"I'm sorry. We're going to take her to feed the ducks," said Beth. "That should calm her down. Where is she?"

"Good luck with that. She's in her room. She said she was going to take a nap."

Evie sat with Kelsey while Beth went down the hall.

"You going to be okay?"

"Of course," said Kelsey. "This fucking Alzheimer's is a bitch. Some days are okay. Some suck royally. There are no good days. Man, if I ever get it, take me out back and shoot me, please."

"Beth would take care of you. You know that."

"Beth. The fucking savior. She's not perfect. You know that. She just sold this place out from under Mama's feet. We need to deal with her in a new place. Talk about sucking."

"Kelsey, she did what was best for everyone involved. If the bank had gotten to you before I did, you'd be out on the street."

"Whatever."

"And the house she found y'all is really cute."

"You've seen it?"

"Yep. She showed it to me before we came here."

"Lucky you," said Kelsey.

Evie heard footsteps approaching. She recognized Beth's sure, strong strides and assumed the shuffling belonged to their mom.

"You ready to go feed ducks?" Beth said.

"Ready as I'll ever be." Evie stood. "You remember me, Mrs. Richards? I'm a friend of Beth's and Kelsey's."

Mama looked blankly at her.

"Are you taking us to the ducks?"

"I am."

"Thank you. Can we go now?"

"Of course. We'll take my car."

CHAPTER TWELVE

Beth was impressed at how at ease Evie seemed. She chatted with Mama and made her laugh. Beth was anything but at ease. She needed more of Evie's kisses, and she was working furiously in her mind trying to figure out when she might get them.

Mama sat on the bench surrounded by ducks, throwing birdseed to them.

"We used to use bread," Mama said.

"That's not good for the ducks," Beth said.

"Sure it is. But they like these seeds just fine."

"They really do," said Evie. "You're their favorite person."

"I am, aren't I?" Mama positively beamed. "And who are you?"

"Me? I'm Evie. I'm a friend of Beth's and Kelsey's."

"You're my friend now, too."

"Thank you," Evie said. "I'd like that."

Beth was amazed at how well things were going. But would Evie be able to hold Mama's attention while she and Kelsey emptied the house tomorrow?

"What's that?" Mama tensed.

"What's what?" Beth said.

"There's smoke over there."

"I don't see any."

"Sure," said Mama. "It's right there."

The sky was a clear blue without any clouds. Beth felt bad for Mama seeing things that weren't there. Especially terrifying things.

"We'd better pack up then," Evie said.

"We need to tell someone," said Mama.

"Mama, there's no smoke," Beth said gently.

"There is! I can see it."

"Let's drive over there," said Evie. "So we'll know exactly where it is when we call it in."

Beth stared at Evie, dumbfounded. Was she really going to drive around the lake for no reason?"

"Good idea," Mama said. "Let's drive over there."

They drove about a quarter of the way around the lake. Evie pulled into a parking lot.

"Does this look like a good place to feed some ducks?"

"Oh, yes," said Mama. "Let's feed some ducks."

Beth climbed out of the back seat of the car.

"Thank you," she mouthed to Evie, who smiled at her. Then winked. Beth melted on the inside.

Beth hovered while Evie kept a constant conversation going with Mama. They started talking about ducks, then Evie steered the conversation to Mama's childhood. Beth had heard all the stories but enjoyed them through Evie's ears.

It was getting dark, so Beth suggested they head back to the house.

"It's getting cold, and I don't have a jacket," was Mama's response.

"The house will be warm, and you won't need a jacket there," Evie said.

They got Mama in the car and drove back to the house. They got her in the house and settled at the dining room table. Kelsey was in the kitchen making dinner.

"I'd better get going," Evie said.

"Stay for dinner," said Kelsey. "There's plenty."

"Thanks, but I've got some things to do."

"I'll walk you to your car," Beth said.

"I think your mom and I are going to be just fine tomorrow."

"I really appreciate you doing that." Beth stood with her hands in her pockets lest she reach out and touch Evie.

"Thanks for everything today, Beth. It's been a really special day."

"Mm-hm."

"So I'll be here around eight tomorrow?"

"Please. Shit. I still need to rent a U-Haul."

"Let me take care of that. You just focus on Mama."

"Thank you. I appreciate it."

"My pleasure. When it comes to you, Beth, everything is my pleasure."

"I wish I could kiss you," Beth whispered.

"Mm. As do I. We'll figure something out. I'm not leaving town without kissing you again."

Beth's heart galloped anew. The fact that Evie was as into her as she was into Evie made everything right in the world. The fact that Evie was really going back to Dallas made everything wrong. Beth hated that.

"Hug me good-bye," Evie said.

Beth took Evie in her arms and held her tight. She smelled Evie's hair, her skin. She committed those scents to memory. She'd never, ever forget how good Evie smelled.

"I'll see you in the morning," Beth whispered in Evie's ear.

"Yes, you will. Eight o'clock sharp. Now let go of me before I throw you in the car and take you with me."

Beth stepped back.

"Promises, promises."

Evie laughed at that, which added more fuel to the fire that threatened to consume Beth's body. Beth watched Evie drive off before going into the house for dinner.

"You and Evie sure have gotten close," said Kelsey.

"Yeah. I guess she's not the devil incarnate after all."

"I'm glad to hear that. I think she's pretty cool."

"That she is. Where's Mama?"

"She had to use the restroom," Kelsey said.

"We need to talk about tomorrow."

"Yeah. It would be nice if I had a clue about what was happening."

"Sorry it's all happened so fast. So at eight tomorrow, Evie is going to come over to keep Mama occupied."

Mama walked into the dining room then. Kelsey served dinner.

"Did you like our friend Evie?" said Kelsey.

"Who?"

"The woman who took us to feed the ducks," Beth said.

"Ducks? I haven't fed the ducks in so long. Can we do that tomorrow?"

"Sure, Mama. You'll get to feed the ducks tomorrow."

Her face brightened.

"Thank you. I love feeding ducks. Will we go to the lake?"

"Sure, Mama," Kelsey said. "Tomorrow will be a day of adventures."

"That sounds lovely. I'm going to bed now."

"You hardly touched your dinner," said Beth.

"I'm not hungry."

"Then you'll need to drink an Ensure."

"Fine. I'll eat a few more bites."

When Kelsey and Beth were okay with the amount of food Mama had eaten, Mama went down the hall for the night.

"So what's the plan for the morning?" said Kelsey.

"Evie will be here at eight to take Mama away. We'll start moving things. First thing will be Mama's bedroom and bath so we can set it up exactly the same at the new place."

"You think she's not going to notice?"

"She'll notice, but keeping things set up much the same as they are here should reduce the confusion and agitation."

"I get what you're saying. Are you sure we have to do this?"

"I'm positive. We have no choice, Kelsey."

❖

Evie woke the next morning excited for the day ahead. Beth and Kelsey would be working hard, but Evie would be with them in spirit. She'd ordered a U-Haul to be delivered at nine thirty, which should give her plenty of time to get Mama to the lake.

She stopped at the grocery store on the way and got an ice chest that she filled with sandwiches and drinks. She and Mama were going to have a great day. And hopefully, if Beth wasn't exhausted later, she was hoping to take her out to celebrate.

Evie pulled up in front of the farmhouse at eight o'clock sharp. She knocked on the door and Kelsey opened it. Evie hoped her disappointment that it hadn't been Beth wasn't written all over her face.

"Hi, Kelsey."

"Good morning. Come on in. Coffee's ready and I'm about to serve breakfast."

"Perfect timing then."

Evie followed Kelsey into the dining room. Still no sign of Beth. Evie couldn't believe how much that upset her. She seriously needed to get a grip.

"Where's Mama?" Evie said.

"She's in her room. Beth is trying to get her dressed. She says she doesn't want to go to the lake. She wants to lie in bed. Says she doesn't feel good."

"Is she okay? Does she need to see a doctor?"

"No. This is her MO. She'll be fine."

Evie heard Beth approaching and told herself to keep calm, but her whole body buzzed in anticipation. Beth smiled when she saw Evie and greeted her with a hug.

"Y'all make a cute couple," Kelsey said.

"What?" snapped Beth.

"What, what? It's not a bad thing. I'm just saying you two would look good as an item. Jeez. Calm down. Where's Mama?"

"She's brushing her teeth. I got her dressed, but it wasn't easy."

"Thanks for handling that," said Kelsey. "Come on, you two. Sit down. Breakfast is ready."

"About that coffee?" Evie said.

"I'll get it for you," said Beth. She set the milk and sugar on the table then brought Evie a cup of coffee.

"I'm going to check on Mama," said Kelsey.

Beth sat next to Evie and placed her hand on her thigh. She gave it a little squeeze before pulling away.

"Beth!" Kelsey called from down the hall. Beth hurried back to Mama's room. She was lying on the floor, groaning.

Beth got her up and situated her on the bed.

"Mama? Tell me what hurts."

"Everything."

"Okay," said Beth. "We'll take you to the ER."

"I don't need a hospital. I just need to rest for a minute."

Evie watched the exchange from the bedroom door. No one seemed to notice she was there. The caring and compassion that Beth showed her terrified mom made Evie's heart swell with pride.

Mama glanced at the door and saw Evie standing there.

"Who are you?"

"That's our friend, Evie," said Kelsey.

"You look nice," Mama said.

"She is," said Beth.

"Do I need to go to the hospital?" Mama asked Evie.

"Do you hurt?" Mama nodded. "Then let's get you checked out. Kelsey and I will take you."

"I need to take her," Beth said.

"You have things you need to take care of," Evie said softly.

Beth glared at Evie, then nodded.

"You're right. Of course. Y'all take her."

They got Mama in the Mercedes and Kelsey directed Evie to the hospital. When they stepped into the ER, the woman at the counter told them only one visitor could go in.

"But I have a mask," Evie pointed out the obvious.

"Sorry. Hospital policy."

"I'll wait in the car."

The wait was interminable. Evie shot Beth a text.

They only let Kelsey in. Should I come help you while I wait?

That would be great.

On my way.

Evie texted Kelsey to let her know when they were ready then headed back to the farm. The idea of helping Beth pack didn't really appeal to Evie, but the concept of being with Beth no matter what did.

Beth opened the door for her and Evie stepped inside.

"Hello, gorgeous," Evie said. Beth grinned.

"Hello, sweetheart."

Beth kissed Evie. A tender kiss that soon morphed into an all-out passion display. Evie held on tight as the kiss intensified. She thought she would fall over if she let go. She was crazy about Beth and Beth was making her even crazier.

Evie stepped back, still grasping Beth's shoulders for balance. "We have work to do, babe."

"I know. But kissing you is way more fun."

"Let's do what we can."

"If you insist," said Beth.

Together they boxed up Mama's belongings and loaded them into the U-Haul. They couldn't move the furniture yet since Mama would be home again.

We're almost ready. Evie saw the text from Kelsey.

"I've got to go, babe," she said.

"Okay. Thanks for your help. I'll walk you to your car."

Evie took Beth's hand and felt all was right in the world. They kissed good-bye.

"Can't wait to see you later," Beth said.

"I hear that."

Mama and Kelsey were just leaving the ER when Evie pulled up. Mama was walking gingerly and looked like she was in a lot of pain.

"Is she okay?" Evie asked as they got her in the car.

"Fractured ribs."

"Shit."

"Yeah. They called in some pain pills. You mind swinging by the pharmacy?"

"Sure. No problem."

They got Mama home and seated at the dining room table.

"You going to be okay?" Evie said.

Mama nodded.

"You're a very nice woman. I want my Beth to meet someone like you."

"Beth?" Evie was surprised.

"Yes. She's a lesbian but I don't think she even knows it. It would make her life better if she had a good woman like you."

CHAPTER THIRTEEN

Mama's trip to the hospital threw a monkey wrench in Beth's plans to get her room moved. She stowed boxes of belongings in the U-Haul but didn't make near the progress she'd hoped before they got home. Even with Evie's help.

She made a point of being at the dining room table sipping coffee when they brought Mama home.

"Why's there a moving truck parked in front of our house?" Mama said.

Beth panicked. Damn. She didn't want to tell Mama about the move until it was pretty much over. She had no choice now.

"We're going to be moving, Mama. We'll be living in Vernon so we're closer to your doctors and things," she said.

"I'm not leaving the farm."

"I know how you feel. But the time has come for us to get into town. It just makes sense."

"Not to me," said Mama. "I'm not leaving."

"Mrs. Richards?" Evie said. "Beth and Kelsey have always taken good care of you, haven't they?"

Mama nodded.

"And they'll continue to do that only from a new house in Vernon. You're going to love it there."

"I won't. And who are you? Why are you here? What business is it of yours?"

"Mama," said Kelsey. "This is our friend Evie. She's been helping us with a lot. She's practically family now."

"You're pretty, Evie. Have you met Beth?"

Beth breathed a sigh of relief. Mama had lost her train of thought which was a really good thing at the moment.

"I have," said Evie.

"Do you like her? She's cute, isn't she?"

"She is indeed. And I like her very much."

Mama smiled and nodded.

"I think I'd like to lie down. I'm a little sore today."

"I'll help you get settled in." Kelsey walked down the hall with her mom.

"You like me very much, huh?" Beth grinned at Evie.

"*Very* much." She winked at Beth.

"Right on."

"So how much did you get loaded into the truck? Enough to make a trip?"

"I suppose so."

"You suppose so what?" Kelsey walked back into the dining room.

"I suppose I have enough stuff to make a trip to the new place."

"I want to see this new place. Can I go with you?"

"Who's going to stay with Mama then?" said Beth.

"I'll stay," Evie said. "She should sleep for a while anyway now, right?"

"True. Okay, Kels, come on. Let's do this."

"So what's going on with you and Evie?" Kelsey said as they drove to town.

"Nothing. Why?"

"I don't know. I just sense something has changed."

"Well, keep your sense to yourself. Nothing has changed except maybe I don't want to kill her anymore."

"That's a definite bonus."

"Indeed."

"We're not in a very nice neighborhood, are we?" said Kelsey.

"It's not bad. We have to go through some not nice areas to get there. But our neighborhood is nice and our house is adorable."

She pulled up in front of the house and Kelsey squealed.

"It's so cute. Oh, Beth. You did good."

"Thanks. Now help me unload these boxes please."

They got the truck unloaded and Beth gave Kelsey a tour of the house.

"I love it. It's perfect," said Kelsey.

"I thought so. Now, we'd better get back. I really don't want Mama waking up while Evie is alone with her."

"Plus you don't want to be away from your new BFF for too long."

"She's your BFF. Not mine." Beth's tone was gruffer than she'd intended, but it was out now. She climbed in the U-Haul.

"If she's not just a new best friend, what is she?"

"Just because I don't want to kill her anymore doesn't make her my best friend. Not by any stretch."

Kelsey laughed.

"Denial isn't just a river in Egypt."

"I'm not denying anything. Now, change the fucking subject. Damn."

They rode back to the house in silence. Beth was filled with mixed emotions. She was fuming at Kelsey for trying to guess what was going on with Evie and her. And she was excited because in a few short minutes, she'd be back with Evie. And then there was the frustration in that she wanted to kiss Evie desperately but wouldn't be able to.

The emotion that rose to the top as she pulled in front of the farmhouse was the anticipation of seeing Evie again. She was beautiful, intelligent, strong, and a great kisser. Beth decided she was everything Beth would have been looking for had she known she was looking for a woman.

Beth followed Kelsey to the dining room and her heart sank when Evie wasn't there.

"They're not in the living room, either," said Kelsey.

"I'll check Mama's room."

She found Evie sitting on the edge of the bed gently rubbing Mama's back. Beth turned to leave them alone, but Evie spoke.

"She's sleeping now. She had a nightmare. I got her calmed down."

"Thank you for that."

Evie smiled at Beth.

"My pleasure." She crossed the room to the doorway where Beth stood. "How'd everything go with you and Kelsey?"

"We got her things hung in the closet. Left some boxes in our rooms that we'll need to put in her dressers when we get them there. But it was a good trip."

"And how does Kelsey like the place?"

"She loves it."

"Oh, Beth. That makes me so happy."

Evie stood there, inches from Beth, and the desire to kiss her was too much. She lowered her lips and claimed Beth's in a brief kiss that caused her soul to shudder.

Beth quickly stepped back.

"Not in front of my mom."

"She's asleep."

But Evie appreciated Beth's cautious side. She did wonder if Beth would ever be able to come out to her mom. She wondered if she should tell her her mom knew Beth was a lesbian. But it wasn't her place. She'd have to be patient with Beth.

"Come on," Evie said. "Let's go find Kelsey."

They found Kelsey in the kitchen.

"I take it you found Mama?" Kelsey said.

"Yeah. She's in bed. She seems to be sleeping well."

"Good. Thanks again for agreeing to stay with her today, Evie. I really appreciate that."

"I understand you loved your new house?"

"Oh, my God. It's adorable. I think Mama's going to like it, too."

"I'm sure she will," said Evie. "Beth did a really good job."

"That she did."

"Thanks. I just hope moving Mama goes smoothly," said Beth.

"I don't know about smooth, but I don't think it'll be too traumatic," said Evie.

"I hope you're right. Do we have any beer in this house?" Beth gazed into the almost empty refrigerator.

"I don't think so. You want me to go buy some?" Kelsey said.

"We can go," said Evie. "Come on, Beth."

Evie took Beth's hand as soon as they were in the car.

"I really like you, Beth. And I'm sorry I kissed you in your mom's room. You're just so damned hard to resist."

Beth laughed.

"I like you, too." She gave Evie's hand a squeeze. "And it's okay. It was a nice kiss."

"You have to know how hard it is not to drag you into a bedroom and have my way with you."

"Is that right?" Beth's eyes grew wide.

"Don't worry. I'm not going to do anything until you're ready. I just thought you might want to know."

"I feel like I'm ready now."

"I appreciate that, but don't think you are. It'll happen. I'm sure of that. And when it does, it's going to be amazing. But I can be patient."

"Thank you for that."

They picked up some beer for Beth, some wine for Kelsey and Evie, and a couple of rotisserie chickens. Evie insisted they buy a premixed salad, too. They got to the register and Beth reached for her wallet.

"Oh, no. This is on me," said Evie.

"Thanks. But we're not charity cases."

"I didn't say you were. I just like to do things for you, Beth. Please let me."

"Fine."

Evie paid but knew Beth was anything but fine.

"I'm sorry," she said in the car. "I just really enjoy taking care of you. You need to get used to that if we're going to go the distance. You don't always need to be the provider, the strong one. I can help carry the load."

"That's going to take some getting used to."

"I get that but try. Pease?"

"I will."

"Thank you. Now, we're almost home. May I hold your hand again?"

They held hands the rest of the way home. Evie knew Beth needed some work. She was far from perfect. But then, so was Evie. They'd evolve together, she decided.

Beth popped the top off a beer while Kelsey poured the wine. Evie grabbed the Trivial Pursuit game and set up at the dining room table.

"Y'all want to be punished?" Beth laughed.

"I'm going to get some new versions of the game. Ones you won't have the answers memorized."

"Is that why I always win?" said Beth.

"Indeed," Kelsey said.

"Whatever. Let's do this."

They were well into the game an hour later. Beth had four pies while Evie and Kelsey had three each. They were laughing at an answer Beth missed when Evie heard something. She held up her hand.

"Sh," she said. "I heard something."

Sure enough, Mama had shuffled down the hall and was in the kitchen. Beth jumped up and was at Mama's side in a second.

"You okay?" Beth said.

"I'm fine. Who are these people in my house?"

"We're your family, Mama."

"My family is dead. My mammy and pappy and husband. All dead. Am I dead?"

"No, Mama. You're not dead. You're very much alive. Now come to the table and sit with us."

"I don't feel good. I'm really sore. Are you a nurse? Can you help with that?"

"I'm not a nurse. I'm your daughter, Beth. But I'll get you something to take for the pain."

"Thank you."

Beth got Mama seated at the table then disappeared down the hall.

"Did you have a good sleep, Mrs. Richards?" said Evie.

"I did. Good morning. What are we having for breakfast?"

"It's afternoon. Almost time for dinner," said Kelsey.

"It can't be. I just woke up."

"You had a little nap," Evie said.

"It feels like morning to me."

Beth was back with Mama's pain pills.

"You're just a little confused because you just woke up," she said. "Now take these. They'll help with the pain."

"What were you three doing? Are you playing a game?"

"Yes," said Beth. "But we'll put it away now."

"No, please don't. I'd love to watch you play."

"Sounds good," said Evie. "We'll keep playing then. Can I get you something to drink?"

"I'd love some coffee."

"I'll get some going for you," Kelsey said.

When Mama had her coffee, they resumed their game. Beth ended up winning, as usual. Evie, competitive though she was, didn't begrudge Beth's victory. She was happy for her. Which was very unusual for her. Yes. She had it bad.

"Mrs. Richards?" Evie said.

"Yes?"

"If you're feeling better tomorrow, I'd like to take you to feed the ducks. Would you like that?"

Mama beamed.

"I'd love that. Thank you. Are you one of my daughters, too?"

"No, ma'am. I'm just a friend of the family. But I'd like to spend the day with you at the lake."

"That would be wonderful. Thank you."

CHAPTER FOURTEEN

Beth worked hard all the next morning getting Mama's room moved and set up in the new house. Kelsey helped with the heavy lifting to the best of her ability. But most of it fell to Beth who, fortunately, was used to hard work.

They took a break around one and drove over to the lake to check on Evie and Mama. They found them sitting at a picnic table, eating lunch.

"This looks cozy," said Beth.

"Hi," Evie said. "We're having fun."

"How are you feeling, Mama?"

She stared blankly at Beth, clearly not recognizing her.

"Are these friends of yours?" Mama asked Evie.

"Oh, yes. Very dear friends." To Beth and Kelsey, she said, "There have been some complaints of pain, but mostly we're doing okay. Not sure how much longer I can keep her entertained though."

"Her room is set up if you want to take her to the new house," said Kelsey.

"How about you let me know when the dining room is set up? And then I'll bring her over."

"Sounds good. We'd better get back to it," Beth said. "I'll text you."

"Okay, ba—Beth. That'll be great."

Beth winked at her, smiled, and turned back to the truck.

They moved the dining room table and hutch, then got it all set up in the new house. It was different, of course, but Beth had high hopes her mama wouldn't notice. She didn't want to add to her confusion, but she also needed to do this.

Dining room is set up. Can you hang with her here until we get our bedrooms set up?

She waited on Evie's reply.

Sure. Can I help with your room? Wink, wink.

Any time. You know that.

We're on our way.

"They're heading here now," Beth told Kelsey.

"Good. I'm going to work in my bedroom."

"Sounds like a plan."

Beth unpacked the kitchen, putting everything as close to where it had been at the old house as possible. She broke down the boxes and put them in the detached garage. She was tired. She was sore. She couldn't wait to see Evie again.

She heard the Mercedes in the driveway and hurried out to meet them. Mama couldn't get out of the car by herself, so Beth helped her out while Evie got her walker from the back seat.

"Where am I?" said Mama.

"You're home, Mama," said Beth.

"I live here?"

"Yep."

"I don't remember. Can you help me inside?"

"Of course."

Mama sat at the dining room table and Evie and Beth sat with her. Beth noticed tears in her mama's eyes.

"What's wrong, Mama?"

"I don't remember this place at all. Am I getting that bad?"

Beth looked over at Evie who shrugged. Shit. What to do?

"This is our new home, Mama," Beth said. "That's why it's not familiar. But we'll make lots of memories here. I promise."

"New? Where did we used to live?"

Evie took Mama's hands in hers.

"You used to live on a farm."

"Pappy's farm," Mama said.

"Exactly. Now you live here. In town. Where it'll be easier to get to places like the store, the hospital. You understand?"

"Where's my pappy?"

Evie looked to Beth with pleading eyes.

"He'll be here later," Beth said. "Do you want to see your room?"

"Yes. And I hurt. I just want to lie down."

Beth gave Mama a pain pill then walked her down the hall to her new room.

"I'm going to like it here," Mama said before lying down. "It's nice."

"Call me if you need me," Beth said.

But Mama's eyes were already closed. Beth and Evie went to Kelsey's room. Kelsey was unpacking boxes and setting up knickknacks and collectibles.

"We need to bring stuff for the bathroom," Kelsey said. "I don't know about you, but I need a long soak in a hot tub."

"I'll go get them."

"No. I will. I need some time."

"Fair enough," Beth said.

With Kelsey gone and Mama asleep, Beth wanted to take advantage of having Evie alone. She didn't know exactly what she wanted but she knew she wanted something. Evie took her hand.

"Show me your room," she said.

"Not much to show. Just some furniture and a lot of boxes."

"Show me."

Beth took Evie to the room on the other side of the main bathroom.

"See?"

Evie sat on the bed and patted it for Beth to sit next to her. Beth sat, hands folded in her lap. She sat staring at her hands.

"Call me crazy," said Evie. "But this seems like the perfect time for you to kiss me."

Beth looked into Evie's eyes and knew she was right. They had privacy. They were alone. She leaned in until their lips met. Beth's heart pounded against its constraints. Without thinking, she slipped her tongue into Evie's warm, moist mouth and she felt pain between her legs. She started to pull back, but Evie held her close. Evie leaned back on the bed and pulled Beth on top of her.

Beth couldn't begin to describe the feel of Evie's soft breasts pushing against hers. Beth was frantic with need but had no clue how to proceed. She rolled off of Evie and propped herself up on an elbow. She dragged her hand across Evie's stomach.

"Why did you stop?" Evie said.

"I don't know. I feel so stupid. I want…I don't know what I want. But I know I want it. Does that make any sense?"

"Of course it does, babe. Beth, do you want to make love with me?"

Beth lay still, silently contemplating the question.

"Yeah. I think that's what I want. But I don't know how. I don't want to disappoint you. Or have you laugh at me."

"I would never do that. I'll guide you. We'll learn together what our likes and dislikes are."

And Evie meant that.

"I wouldn't know where to begin," said Beth.

"Again, not to worry. You just do what you want, what feels right."

"Now?"

"No," Evie said. "Not until we're properly alone. And have plenty of time to explore each other."

Beth nodded her understanding. Evie was happy when Beth leaned forward and kissed her again. Evie loved Beth's tight stomach against hers, her muscular thighs pressing into her. Everything about Beth felt right.

"Beth?" Evie pushed Beth up when she heard Mama calling. "You'd better go see what's up."

"But my legs feel like jelly. How can I walk?"

"Beth?" Mama called again.

"Don't move. I'll be right back."

But Evie did move. She straightened her clothes and followed Beth down the hall.

"There's my friend," said Mama.

"Hi there," said Evie.

"What do you need, Mama?" Beth said.

"I'm scared."

"Of what?"

"I don't know. I'm just really scared."

"How about if I lie with you until you've fallen back asleep?" Evie said.

"Okay. That would be nice. But why am I scared? Who's coming to get me?"

"No one, Mama. You're safe. I'm here with you. And so's Evie."

"Someone is coming to get me, though."

"Sh," said Evie. "I think you had a bad dream. Lie back down. I'll lie with you. Just relax."

"A bad dream? I don't have bad dreams."

"I think you had one this time, Mama. You sleep now."

"Okay." She snuggled back against Evie who held her gently. It wasn't the Richards woman Evie wanted to be holding in bed, but Evie really cared about Mama. Something about Evie, her cold, hard exterior, was melting. And she wasn't too sure how she felt about that.

Evie actually fell asleep because she awoke a little later and it was dark outside. She carefully disentangled herself from Mama and followed the voices down the hall to the kitchen.

"Hey, Sleeping Beauty," said Kelsey. "How's Mama?"

"Still fast asleep." Evie ran her hands through her hair. "I must look a fright."

"Far from it," said Beth.

Kelsey cast her a side-eyed glance but didn't say a word.

"You look fine," Kelsey said.

"You're both too kind. What are we doing?"

"Finishing up the kitchen and getting ready to order pizza."

"You buy, I'll fly," said Evie.

"They have deliveries nowadays." Kelsey laughed.

"Sure they do. But they won't deliver the beer and wine to go with it."

"You make a valid point. And I could sure go for a beer," said Beth.

"Great. You call in the order and I'll be back in a flash."

"Don't you need to know which pizza place we're ordering from?" said Kelsey.

"Text me. I'll be back."

Evie needed to put some distance between herself and the Richards family. They were dangerous, each in their own way. Kelsey who was a party girl like herself, Mama who was so childlike and confused. And Beth. How did she feel about Beth? Why did it feel so different from any other hookup? Probably because Evie had never been with a virgin before. That must be the reason. Surely it was.

She returned to the house with two bottles of red wine and a twelve-pack of Coors Light that made her shudder to buy. She'd have to introduce Beth to real beer. She couldn't keep drinking that piss water from Colorado.

She went back out to her car and brought in two pizzas. When she got back to the dining room, Mama was up, and Kelsey had opened the wine. She poured three glasses while Beth stood drinking her beer.

"I picked up some paper plates too. No one wants to do dishes tonight," Evie said.

"Amen to that," Kelsey said.

Beth sat at the table and Evie sat as close to her as she could without being obvious. But Kelsey must have noticed. She looked from Beth to Evie and then arched an eyebrow. Evie smiled and that was that.

They ate, drank, and chatted. It was a nice, relaxed evening after a stressful day for all involved.

Evie asked Mama about her younger days and Mama regaled them with stories of her youth and her college days. Evie felt more at home than she ever had. Sure, she had a family, but interactions with them were tense and uncomfortable. Ever since Evie had come out to them when she was nineteen, she'd been shunned. She avoided her family and they avoided her.

Robert's family was much more accepting and that's where she generally spent holidays and such. But she didn't belong there. They had five kids already and Evie felt like an outsider at gatherings.

This family, though. This family made her feel like she belonged. She should have run at that moment, but something made her stay. What the hell was she doing? What was her end game? That was the bottom line in everything she did. What was her end game? She didn't know the answer.

Mama went to bed and Kelsey took a bath.

"What should we do now?" said Beth.

Evie looked at the empty living room. TV was out. Kelsey was in the bath, so making out in Beth's room was out.

"I think it's time for me to say good night," Evie said.

"Yeah?"

"Yeah. I'll be back in the morning to watch Mama while you and Kelsey finish moving."

"Great. I do appreciate you taking care of Mama, you know?"

"I know, babe. Now, kiss me good night."

Beth closed the distance between them. She cupped Evie's jaws and kissed her with more emotion than passion. Evie's heart skipped a beat. What the hell?

"I'll see you tomorrow," Evie said.

"Sounds good. Drive carefully."

Evie was almost to her Airbnb when her phone rang. Hoping it was Beth, she grabbed it. It was Robert. She threw the phone onto the passenger seat. Robert was the last person she needed to talk to at that moment.

Chapter Fifteen

Evie was working a child's puzzle with Mama while Beth and Kelsey got the living room set up. Mama was completely engaged when Beth glanced over at the dining room table. And Evie was watching Beth. Beth's stomach did a somersault. She couldn't believe Evie, Evelyn flippin' Bremer, had turned out to be the woman of her dreams. She'd thought she'd hate her forever. My how things changed. She grinned at Evie.

"Yo, lovergirl," said Kelsey. "How about some help?"

Beth turned away from Evie, glared at Kelsey, then finished setting up the television. She turned it on just as Mama and Evie finished the puzzle.

"Mama? You want to watch some TV?" Kelsey said.

"I want to watch my show."

Beth flipped through the channels until she found one with all day *Family Feud*. Mama loved that show. Mama clapped and beamed at her.

"Oh, thank you, Bethy."

Beth glanced at Evie who mouthed, "Bethy" and raised her eyebrows. Beth tried to scowl at her but couldn't. She laughed instead.

"Hey, Bethy," Evie said. "Shall we go pick up some lunch?"

Kelsey busted out laughing and Beth cast a glare her way. Kelsey blew her a kiss before sitting down on the couch with Mama.

"Y'all go. We'll be here when you get back."

Beth climbed into the Mercedes and took Evie's hand.

"I could get used to riding in this," said Beth.

Evie laughed.

"So, buy a car. Get rid of that truck."

"We have a car. We just don't use it often."

"Well, you don't need the truck anymore. Sell it and buy a new model car. You deserve it."

"We'll see. Where are you going?"

Evie had turned off main street and was driving by some factories.

"You'll see," she said.

Evie parked in a lot behind a dilapidated building.

"This place looks like it's going to fall down any minute. What do you need here?"

"It's deserted all right. Which means there's no one around. Kiss me, Beth. Dear God, I need you to kiss me."

Beth's heart thudded hard. Just the thought of kissing Evie made her crazy. But the actual act? Ecstasy.

She leaned into Evie and they kissed briefly. Beth sat back.

"What?" said Evie. "That's all I get?"

"I didn't know…" Beth looked around.

"There's no one here. Now, kiss me like you mean it."

Beth kissed Evie with more force and soon their mouths opened and their tongues frolicked together. Beth tried to press harder into Evie. Damned seat belt. She got it unlocked and Beth's breath caught when she felt Evie's soft, full breasts against her.

There was that pain between her legs. She squeezed her legs together and shuddered. She knew it had something to do with Evie. She knew it was because she wanted her so desperately. She needed to figure out how to make love to her. And when.

Evie helped Beth into a sitting position.

"We'd better go get food before Kelsey sends out a search party."

Beth nodded. She couldn't find her voice. With shaky hands, she buckled up again.

They picked up lunch and when they walked in the house, Kelsey said, "It's about time. What took so long?"

"Long line," Evie said.

Beth turned around so Kelsey couldn't see the smile on her face.

"Mama?" Evie said. "Do you want to eat here or at the table?"

"Table, please."

Beth set the table and they sat to enjoy their lunch. After, Evie sat in the living room with Mama while Kelsey and Beth headed to the farmhouse for the last load.

"I can't believe we're almost done," Beth said.

"Are you ever going to admit you and Evie are a thing?" said Kelsey.

"What are you talking about?"

"Look, you're a lesbian. No shock there. And I think y'all make a cute couple. In other words, I'm one hundred percent supportive. So just fess up."

"Again. No clue what you're talking about."

They rode the rest of the way in silence. When they got the odds and ends loaded in the truck, they vacuumed then shampooed the carpets and they were done. It was time to give Evie the keys.

"You okay?" said Kelsey.

"I guess. Kinda bummed, but excited to start our new life."

"I hear ya."

"We should get back."

They found Mama and Evie watching TV. Beth loved watching how Evie interacted with Mama. Even just watching TV, she was engaged with Mama, holding her hand, laughing with her. It made Beth's heart happy.

"Mama," said Evie. "Look who's home."

"Who are they?"

"It's me, Beth, and Kelsey."

Mama shrunk back against the couch.

"Who are you? What are you doing in my friend's house?"

"Mama," said Evie, but Beth shook her head.

"Come on, Kels, let's leave the room for a minute."

"I fuckin' hate when she doesn't recognize us," said Kelsey.

"Yeah. I know. But it's going to happen. And probably more frequently."

"Doesn't mean I have to like it."

"No. No, it doesn't. Let's go out again and see if she recognizes us now."

They walked back out to the living room.

"What are you watching, Mama?" said Beth.

"*Family Feud.*"

"You enjoying yourself?" Mama nodded. "Good. Will you sit quietly while I talk to your friend in the kitchen?"

"Yes."

"Thanks." Beth kissed the top of Mama's head then walked to the kitchen, followed by Evie.

"What's going on?" said Evie. "Should we have left her alone?"

"She'll be fine. Besides, Kelsey's in the living room with her."

"So, we're alone?" Evie wiggled her eyebrows.

"Very funny. No. Here. These are yours now." She dropped the keys to the farmhouse in Evie's hands.

"Thanks, Beth. I know how hard this must be."

"It sucks. But it's time. So take them and let's not talk about them again."

Evie kissed Beth's cheek as she watched Beth blink away tears. Her heart broke for Beth. But this was business. And business always came before pleasure.

"Thank you," was all Evie said. She slid the keys in her pocket. She turned to go back to the living room. When she got there, she realized Beth wasn't with her. She went back to the kitchen to find Beth, elbows on the sink, crying. She tiptoed back to the living room. Clearly Beth needed some privacy.

"Where's my sister?" said Kelsey.

"Not sure. I'm guessing she just needed a few minutes alone."

"She gave you the keys?" Evie nodded. "Gotcha."

Evie left the house shortly thereafter. She felt like an interloper. She felt like she'd completely disrupted the life of this lovely family. She felt like shit.

She drove to Charlie's for a lemon drop. She knew she had to get ready to go back to Dallas. She couldn't ignore Robert's calls forever. He had a right to ask for an update. And now that she had the keys, she could tell him that much.

While Beth and Kelsey had been busy getting moved, Evie had been working behind the scenes, selling the cattle to ranchers in the area. So it was time to move on the demolition. The crops would be tilled under. The windmills would go up. Evie would make a small killing. And she felt like shit.

Damn Beth for being so fucking adorable. Evie had always been a sucker for a hot butch and Beth was certainly all that. She preferred her women confident, secure. And, in her own way, Beth was both of those. Even after Evie had thrown a monkey wrench in her life, Beth had landed on her feet.

Of course, one of the main attractions for any of Evie's bedmates, was they had to be great kissers. And Beth was certainly that. She had saved her first kiss for Evie and each kiss was better, more passionate, more intense, than the one before.

It was time to leave, though. Maybe she'd pack up and leave in the middle of the night. Not because she didn't want to see Beth again, but because of how desperately she did. It wasn't healthy.

She finished her drink and stepped out into the bright sun. Her phone rang and she could barely make out Robert's name.

"Hello?" she said.

"You've been avoiding me."

"Whatever. I'm packing now to head home."

"Good. You've been dillydallying long enough."

"I've been taking care of things. Wrapping up loose ends. But I'm ready. I should be home tomorrow."

"It's about time."

"Good-bye, Robert."

"Good-bye."

"So you'll be home tomorrow?"

She spun to see Beth standing there.

"I need to get home, Beth. You knew this day was coming. Come back to the house with me and let's talk about our future."

"I'll head there right now."

Evie handed her a key.

"Let yourself in. I'll stop and grab you some beer."

"Sounds good."

Evie walked into the house to find Beth at the dining room table, the file on her farm opened in front of her. She stood when Evie entered and her eyes were rock hard.

"You used me," Beth said.

"I didn't."

"You had a whole file on me and my family. You knew everything there was to know about us. You played me like a fiddle."

"Beth, please."

"You can't deny it."

"That file was to help me get you to sell the farm. It has nothing to do with us. You and me. That was completely different."

"I don't see how," said Beth.

"You're upset. You're not thinking clearly. I get that. Of course we had a file on the farm. We have files on all the property we're purchasing. We'd be irresponsible if we didn't. But it wasn't a way to get to know you, Beth. That happened over the course of the purchase. You wormed your way into my heart. It wasn't something I was expecting, but it happened. I can't imagine losing you now."

"You're so full of shit. Listen to yourself. Blah, blah, blah. You targeted me. You're a fuckin' predator. That's what you are. And I fell for it, hook, line, and sinker. You're smooth, Evelyn. I'll give you that much. You knew just what buttons to push and just what to say and do to get me to fall for you. And now? I see that. And I hate you for it. Good-bye, Evelyn."

Evie reached out and grabbed Beth's arm. Beth tried to shake free, but Evie held tight.

"I'm not letting you go like this. It's not like that at all. Now, calm your ass down and let's go over this rationally."

"I'm not going to calm down. And I'm being rational. I can see things more clearly than anything I've seen in the past week or so. Let me go, Evelyn."

"Please, Beth."

"Good-bye."

She jerked her arm free and Evie heard her tires squeal as she drove off into the sunset.

Evie was crushed. She'd foolishly let her heart get involved and now she fought the tears that threatened to spill over. Beth would come around when she calmed down. At least she hoped she would. Evie needed that country bumpkin in her life in a way she'd never needed anyone before.

She got her things together, packed her car, and started the three-hour drive back to Dallas. The drive was uneventful, and she arrived just after eleven.

The view from the twenty-second floor of her high-rise did nothing to quell the loneliness inside her. There was an ache that she was unfamiliar with, but she knew it was because she was back to life and reality. Life and reality which didn't include Beth.

Really though, could she have done a long-distance relationship? Was she cut out for that? She didn't know. All she knew now was that she wanted to try. She sent Beth a text.

I miss you. Please text me back. We can make this work.

The next morning, Evie was up at five and at the gym by five-thirty. She pushed herself hard, harder than ever before, but it didn't stop her brain from thinking.

She showered and dressed in her most powerful power suit. It was a black skirt and jacket with a red silk blouse. She looked good. But she didn't feel good. Damn. She checked her phone. Still no response.

She drove to the office where Robert hugged her tight.

"It's so good to have you back, hon. It feels like you've been gone forever."

Evie hugged him back, but barely.

"Good to be back." She tried to smile, but it wavered as the tears threatened.

"What the hell? Come, sit," said Robert. "Tell me what is going on."

"Nothing to tell. Here are the keys to the farmhouse. It's ready to be torn down."

Robert rubbed his hands together.

"Good job, Evie. That property is a gold mine."

"That it is. I'm going to start working on getting it prepared for demolition now."

"Right on. And, Evie? I don't know what happened up there, but I'm here for you. And I really am glad you're back."

"Thanks, Robert. Let me bury myself in my work and I'll be just fine."

"That's the Evie I know and love."

Evie called a local company in Vernon to have them bulldoze the property in Walker. It would be done later that week and then Evie would be able to get the windmill farm up and running.

She scheduled a meeting with the engineers for later that week. She felt good. She was wheeling and dealing. She was home. She checked her phone. Still no response from Beth. Just like that, she was miserable.

CHAPTER SIXTEEN

"What the hell do you mean you're going back to school? What about Mama? What about me?" Kelsey's voice continued to rise. "I swear, you've turned into the most self-absorbed, mopey, unpleasant person on earth. I don't know what's going on, but you'd better snap out of it."

"Are you through? Because I need to register."

"Beth. Seriously. You're just going to leave me here alone with Mama while you go off to play?"

"Getting a degree in business management is not playing," said Beth.

"Whatever. Are you even listening?"

"I've found a place in town. Like an adult day care for Alzheimer's patients. She can go there while I'm doing my schoolwork."

"And Covid?"

Beth heaved a heavy sigh.

"Look, Kelsey. This is happening. Why don't you go back to school, too? Get a degree?"

"Right."

"Think about it. Surely you want something out of life."

"Sure. I want to get married and have babies."

"Then do it."

"When? How?"

"That I don't know. That's up to you," said Beth.

"I won't abandon Mama just because you do."

"I'm not abandoning anyone. It'll be good for her to get out. It'll stimulate her mind. Trust me."

"I don't trust you. You are the last person I trust." Kelsey stormed out of the room.

Fuckin' women. Can't live with them. Can't shoot them.

Beth opened the laptop to Vernon College's website and registered for classes starting in August. That didn't give her much time. She'd be mostly taking classes online due to the pandemic, but would eventually be in the classroom. She hoped.

She was terrified at the prospect of going back to school. She hadn't ever done well as a student. Ever. But she had to give it her all. She could get her AA then move away after Mama passed and work for a company. She had to do it now. If she got any older, she might not be hirable.

She had no idea what kind of company she wanted to work for. She figured as long as it had nothing to do with windmills, she'd be okay. She was still pissed at Evie but more so at herself for falling so hard for her. What a fool she'd been.

Beth turned her attention back to the laptop. To hell with Evie, she had a future to prepare for. She ordered her books and was set. She closed the laptop and went back to check on Mama.

She heard the muffled sobs as she approached. Mama was crying into her pillow.

"Mama?" she said. "Mama, what's wrong?"

There was no answer, but Beth recognized the smell of urine in the air. She placed her hand on Mama's back.

"Did we have an accident?"

Mama howled like she was in pain. Beth forced herself to remain calm. She couldn't help if she didn't know what the issue was.

"Talk to me, Mama."

"What's going on?" Kelsey was in the doorway. "Mama? Are you okay?"

"Sh," said Beth. "Stay calm until we know what's going on."

Beth pulled back the covers on the bed. Mama was sopping wet. As were her bedclothes.

"I'll get some dry sheets," said Kelsey.

"Mama, it's okay," said Beth. "These things happen. Now let's get you out of your wet clothes."

Mama pulled her knees to her chest and sobbed harder.

"You're going to need to talk to me," said Beth. "Are you hurting? Or just embarrassed? What's going on?"

"It's part of this damned disease, isn't it?" said Mama.

"Hm? Yes. It is. So there's nothing to worry about. Let's get out of that wet nightgown.

She got Mama to the side of the bed and pulled her nightgown over her head. Kelsey was back with clean sheets and some towels. They worked together to get Mama dried off and dressed in dry clothes.

"Promise me something, Beth," Mama said.

"Anything."

"You'll take me to a doctor who can make me better."

"You know I would if I could."

"Please." Mama sounded desperate and pathetic at the same time.

"Let's get you some breakfast while Beth cleans up in here," Kelsey said.

"So, no promise?" Mama said.

"I'm sorry, Mama." Beth willed herself not to cry in front of them. In her own room, later tonight, when she was alone. Then and only then would she allow the tears of frustration to fall.

She got the bed changed and threw the wet sheets and blankets in the washing machine. Kelsey approached her as she washed her hands.

"What's up?" said Beth.

"Maybe we could get more help for in the house. Rather than taking her out of the house. I feel like she'd do better staying at home."

"I disagree. I think she needs stimulation. But if that's the way you want to go, that's the way we'll go. I'll get some helpers for here so you won't have the sole responsibility."

"Thanks, Beth."

"You're welcome." She walked over to the table. "How are you, Mama? What's for breakfast?"

"Will you read to me, Bethy? I feel all out of sorts and would love to relax and have you read to me."

"Of course. I'll get your book. You want to go sit in the easy chair?"

"Yes. I'll be there waiting for you," said Mama.

Beth got *Gone with the Wind* and sat on the couch next to Mama's chair.

"Where shall we start?"

"The beginning, Beth. Start from the beginning, please."

Beth wasn't halfway through the first chapter when she looked up to see Mama sound asleep. Beth closed the book and got out her laptop. She'd need to cancel Mama's place at the daycare and sign her up for home help. Might as well get that done now.

❖

Evie lived and breathed the new windmill farm. It was in her blood and she couldn't wait to get started building it. The team to get permits had been assigned long ago and the study to make sure the farm wouldn't cause a danger to wildlife migrating had happened before Evie ever set foot in Walker.

Now was the time to meet with the lawyers to go over the legal mumbo jumbo. She was ready. Robert had prepped her thoroughly. She wished Robert would have taken this meeting instead of her, but this was her baby. Thus, her meeting.

Her legal consultants specialized in renewable energy development and, when the meeting started, presented Evie with the permits she'd need to proceed.

"You could have told me in an email you had the permits." Evie did not appreciate people wasting her time.

"We didn't know if you'd have any questions."

"I do have one. From a legal standpoint, are we ready to proceed?"

"We are."

"Excellent." She slid the permits in her folder. "Thank you for your time."

Evie was irritated and relieved at the same time. And excited. It was time to work on manufacturing the windmills. They'd be built and shipped to Walker by train.

She told Robert good night and drove to the manufacturing plant. It was a huge, cement building with very few windows. She supposed that was to prevent people from learning secrets. She didn't know though.

She took the elevator to the fifth floor and met with Liza Umberto, who'd been her contact for years. Liza was a formidable woman in her fifties with short salt-and-pepper hair and brown eyes that were cool and calculating.

"Another farm, eh, Evie? Soon you'll own the whole state."

"Just the windy parts." Evie laughed.

"How many windmills do you need and when do you need them?"

"Twenty windmills should do it. And can you have them ready last week?"

"Ha! You're funny." She turned her attention to her computer and scrolled silently while Evie was left to cool her jets. "I can have them done by November twelfth. Not a minute sooner."

"November twelfth it is. Thank you for your time."

"Evie?"

"Hm?"

"Would you like a drink? It is Friday, after all. Or were you heading back to the office?"

"No office for me. I'd love a drink."

"Great. I know a little place not far from here. You can follow me."

Evie parked next to Liza's Jag in front of a strip mall.

"I don't think I've ever been in a bar in a strip mall," said Evie.

"This place is great. Strong drinks and there's never anyone in here. I don't know how it stays open."

Evie was intrigued as Liza held the door open for her. The place was well lit and the walls were covered with Dallas Cowboy memorabilia. It was a very comfortable place, and, as Liza promised, it was empty.

"Seven and Seven," Liza told the bartender. She looked at Evie. "And?"

"I'll have a lemon drop martini, please."

They got comfortable at a booth along the wall.

"Seven and Seven?" Evie laughed. "Are you for real?"

"It's been my drink for over forty years now. Why mess with a good thing?"

Evie shook her head and laughed. She raised her glass, "To good things."

Liza tapped Evie's glass.

"Indeed."

Evie was thoroughly enjoying Liza's stories of how she used to be a hellion. By the time she finished her second lemon drop, she was completely relaxed.

"And you, Evie?" said Liza. "Have you always been a well-behaved woman?"

"Ah. Far from it. Though I'd rather not share my hell-raising past with a colleague."

"Come on. I showed you mine. You show me yours."

Something in the way she said it more than the words themselves caused Evie's stomach to flip. She felt a pulsing between her legs. Was Liza hitting on her?

"One more drink," said Liza. "Then we'll call it good."

When she came back with the drinks, she sat next to Evie rather than across from her.

"So tell me," Liza said. "How did a beautiful young woman such as yourself get interested in windmills? I have to say, that's quite an unusual obsession."

"They're necessary. I don't like oil, coal, you know. Fossil fuels. They're killing our planet. We need alternatives and I chose windmills."

Liza nodded.

"I'm glad. That's awesome. I agree with you one hundred percent."

"Thank you."

"I've got to level with you, Evie. I find you incredibly attractive. Tell me you don't have a husband or boyfriend waiting for you?"

"None of the above." Evie shook her head. She was finding it hard to breathe. The sexual tension between Liza and herself was thick. Evie had never been with anybody Liza's age but had no doubt Liza could teach her a thing or two. And Evie was always an eager student.

"Girlfriend? Wife?"

"I'm single."

"And which way does your wind blow?" said Liza.

"I play on your team."

"Excellent. This makes me very happy. There's a hotel just down the street. You want to follow me?"

"Of course."

The room was nice. It had a king-sized bed and a decent view of the city.

"Are you going to stare out that window all night?" Liza nibbled on Evie's neck. Evie spun around and captured Liza's lips in a powerful, passionate kiss.

Damn, Liza could kiss. Liza untucked Evie's blouse and unbuttoned it.

"Ah. Skimpy red satin bra. I should have known," Liza said. She kneaded Evie's breast and teased her nipple through her bra.

Shit. Evie was teetering. She was so close just from this play. She needed to get a grip. She couldn't come too soon. She hadn't had any relief in a long time, though. Not since Beth got her all hot and bothered and then Evie had fucked things up.

Beth. She'd really cared for her. She didn't care for Liza. What was she doing?

"I'm sorry," Evie said. "I'm really sorry. But I can't do this. I thought I could. I really did. But I'm just not ready."

"You want to talk about it?"

"No. Thanks, Liza. Maybe another time?"

"I'm always up for it."

"Thanks again." Evie got herself together and, on shaky legs, made it to the lobby and out to her car. Fuck you, Beth. How dare she rear her head at a time like that? Would Evie ever be able to just get laid again?

CHAPTER SEVENTEEN

Beth was struggling and she was only taking prerequisites. How in the hell did she think she'd do once she got into the nitty-gritty of her major? She was doing okay in Algebra and Government, but Composition was killing her, and Public Speaking terrified her. She was only a month in and was maintaining a C average. She needed to step it up. Big time.

"I really don't like Isabel," said Kelsey.

"What?" Beth hated to be interrupted when she was studying.

"Isabel. That woman you hired. I don't like her."

Beth closed her laptop, accepting this was going to be a long, drawn-out conversation.

"What's wrong with her?"

"She's lazy. And she's always on her phone."

"What do you mean?"

"If you paid attention, you'd know this already," Kelsey said.

"Kelsey, I'm in school. That's where my attention is. Not here. You're in charge of making sure things are running smoothly."

"Okay. Well, I'm telling you. They're not going well, and we need to make some changes."

"What changes would you like me to make?" Beth fought to not let her frustration show.

"Get rid of Isabel. Bring in someone new."

"Are you sure it wouldn't be easier to take her to that day care place?"

"I don't know. Beth, can we talk? Can you focus?"

"I am focused." Beth clasped her hands on her desk. "Talk to me."

"Mama misses you. She asks for you all the time."

"Look, school is taking a lot of time. But I have to do it. I need to do something with my life. I'll try to be more present to Mama and you though."

"Thank you. Come out of your room once in a while."

"If you want to know the truth, Kelsey, school is kicking my ass. I need more time to study, not less."

"Seriously?" said Kelsey.

"Yeah. I'm not doing well. I'm thinking of getting a tutor."

"You're determined to blow through that money Evie gave us, aren't you?"

The sound of her name did something to Beth. She felt like she'd been punched in the gut. She fought to maintain composure.

"That reminds me," Beth said. "I have a meeting with a financial advisor in an hour. I'll come out to the dining room and see what Isabel is doing."

"Thank you."

Isabel was so engrossed in her phone, she didn't even notice Beth and Kelsey come in.

"If you could save your phone time for when you're not caring for my mom, that would be great," said Beth.

Mama was staring out the back door, lost in her own world.

"Mama," Beth said. "Isabel is going to work a puzzle with you, okay?"

Mama smiled.

"That would be nice."

"I'll help," said Kelsey.

"What about you, Bethy?" Mama said.

"I've got a meeting. I've got to get ready to go. I'll work one with you when I get home, okay?"

"Okay. You're busy. I know that."

"Never too busy for you though. Remember that." She kissed Mama's paper-thin cheek. "I love you, Mama."

Beth still had a chunk of change left from Evelyn. Even after the house, school, and the caregivers. She and the financial advisors looked at a realistic budget for Kelsey, Mama, and herself.

"What about emergencies? We should probably have a slush fund for you. But you can't touch it unless it's an emergency. Do you understand?"

"I do," Beth said. "We shouldn't have any emergencies, but I get what you're saying."

He spun his monitor to show Beth how much she had left to play with. Beth let out a low whistle.

"So, let's invest," she said.

"Great. I'll put together a portfolio for you. This money will grow. I can almost guarantee it."

"Almost?"

He laughed.

"I can't guarantee anything in reality. But I'm quite confident you'll have a nice little nest egg whenever you need it."

"Thank you so much."

"You're quite welcome. It's been a pleasure, Ms. Richards."

"Indeed." She shook his hand and had a spring in her step as she walked back out to her car. Her phone buzzed and she saw it was from Kelsey.

Isabel just quit.

Why?

Mama had an accident and Isabel wouldn't clean her up.

Shit.

Exactly.

I'm on my way home.

Damn it. She didn't need this headache. How hard was it to clean up a little pee? If everything Kelsey said was true, it was good riddance anyway. She called the agency before she started the car and requested a call back from the head of scheduling.

She got home and found Kelsey sitting at the dining room table.

"Where's Mama?" said Beth.

"She's embarrassed, so she went to bed."

"Poor thing."

"Tell me. I got her clean and got the hallway clean. I still smell poop though."

"What?" Beth raised her eyebrows. "It was that kind of accident?"

Kelsey nodded.

Beth ran her hand over her hair. Were they entering the incontinence stage? Or were these flukes? She wished she knew.

"What are we going to do, Beth?"

"I don't know." Her phone rang. It was Jill from the agency. "Hello?"

"Hi, Beth. I understand Isabel left mid-shift today. I'm so sorry."

"That's okay. I'm a little concerned that we may need more help, though. Mama's been incontinent a couple of times today. Do you have anybody who can handle accidents?"

"I think it's time you get a licensed caregiver there. Like a CNA. Or a home health aide. I'd talk to your mom's doctor. I'm afraid we just have private caregivers for light housekeeping and companionship. I'm really sorry, Beth."

"That's okay," Beth said again. "Thanks for calling anyway."

"What?" said Kelsey.

"We need to get like a home health aide or something like that. I need to get her in to see her doctor."

"Can we afford that?"

"I think Medicare pays for that. But I'm not sure. Wait. She has long term insurance from Pappy. I'm sure they'd cover that."

"Maybe it's time for that day care. Surely they have people on staff who can help?"

"I'll see if they have any openings. Shit. I need to study. I'll call the day care first."

They had an opening and Beth would bring Mama first thing in the morning.

"What am I going to do while she's gone all day? I can't just eat bon bons and watch soap operas."

"You could go back to school. Or you could be in charge of the house."

"School is stupid. No offense. I'll be the stay-at-home house sister. And I'll be the best damned one around."

"Thanks, Kels. I appreciate that."

❖

October arrived and with it, more chores for Evie. They were a month away from the windmills being ready. It was time to dig the holes and fill them with reinforced concrete to serve as a stabilizing foundation.

The terrain wasn't rocky, so it shouldn't be a problem. It did mean that Evie would be going back to Vernon to supervise the work in Walker. Sure, the foreman would be calling the shots, but if there were any questions or logistical problems, Evie would have to be there to answer them.

She wanted to reach out to Beth but knew her text would go unanswered. Just as the myriad texts she'd sent over the past months had. She couldn't believe how Beth had taken hold in Evie's heart. That place was off limits. Always had been. But that's where Beth resided, and Evie had to do something to exorcise her.

She'd been too focused on the project to enjoy the company of a woman. With the exception of the close call with Liza. How dare Beth rob her of pleasure? They'd never even slept together. So why the feeling that Liza would have meant she'd cheated on Beth?

Closure. That's what she needed. And that's what she'd get. The first night back in Vernon, Evie set her things down then drove immediately to Catfish Charlie's.

"Long time no see, city slicker," said Charlie. "You want a lemon drop?"

"Please." When it was served, she asked Charlie, "Has Beth been by today?"

"Beth's been gone damned near as long as you have. Last I heard, she was in school and didn't have time for her ol' pal Charlie."

"School, huh? Good for her."

"Oh my God! I thought that was your car out there."

Evie turned to see Kelsey standing, arms open. She hugged her and tried not to think about Kelsey's sister's arms around her. She just relaxed in the moment.

"How are you?" said Kelsey.

"I'm well, thanks. And you?"

"Ready for a drink or ten." She laughed.

Evie waited until Kelsey had her drink.

"How's Mama?"

"I don't know. She's declining. It's getting hard."

"I'm sorry. Is it just you and Beth caring for her still?"

"Beth's in school now so she takes Mama to a day care during the day. She seems to enjoy it according to the staff. Of course, she doesn't remember any of it by the time she gets home."

"I'm sorry, Kelsey," said Evie.

"Thanks. It sucks. She's going downhill and I hate to think that we're getting close, you know?"

"I can't imagine."

"On other not-so-happy fronts, will you be reaching out to Beth?"

"She's not answering my texts, so no."

"Bummer. She's been moping around since you left town," said Kelsey.

That made Evie feel good. She ducked her head to hide her smile.

"Well, while I'm sorry to hear that, there's nothing I can do to help since she won't talk to me."

"Come over to the house. That way she'd have to talk to you."

"Danger, Kelsey. Though I do like the way you think."

"Seriously." Kelsey spun on her barstool to face Evie. "Why not? Look, I don't know what happened between you two, but I have my suspicions. If you want to see her, you'll have to come to the house."

"Okay. I will."

"Great. Let's go."

"Not tonight. Not tomorrow. I'm going to be in town a while. I'll make it there. I promise."

"Okay. So what brings you back to our little hole in the wall?" Kelsey said.

"It's time to get ready for the windmills. They'll be done next month, and I want to be sure the footings are in place."

"You and those damned windmills."

Evie laughed.

"They're my life."

"I guess."

"What about you, Kelsey? What have you been up to? Beth's in school. Mama's in day care. What are you up to? Are you in school, too?"

"Not me." Kelsey ordered them each another drink. "School is the last thing I need. I take care of the house. That's about it."

"That doesn't sound too fulfilling."

"It's good practice. I'm going to be a housewife someday."

"That's your goal in life?" said Evie.

"It is."

Evie didn't understand, but she couldn't knock it. Not everybody had lofty goals and aspirations. There was nothing wrong with being a housewife. She supposed someone had to do it. She was just glad it wasn't her.

"And are you actively looking for Mr. Right?" she said.

"Not yet. I've got my hands full at home. Someday though. Hopefully soon. I can't wait to get married and have babies. What about you, Evie? Are you ever going to settle down?"

Evie took a sip of her lemon drop as she contemplated her answer.

"I do believe that ship has sailed, unfortunately."

"What do you mean?" said Kelsey. "You're not too old. Surely Ms. Right is out there somewhere?"

"Maybe. I just have a hard time believing it's going to happen for me."

"Maybe you need to make it happen."

"Maybe."

"I've got to go. Don't be a stranger, okay? And for fuck's sake, come by the house."

"I will." And, this time when she said it, she almost believed she would. "As soon as things calm down."

"Sounds good. Should I give Beth your love?" Kelsey laughed.

"I don't think that would go over very well."

Kelsey shrugged.

"It's worth a shot. It's good seeing you. I'm glad you're back in town."

"Too bad everyone doesn't feel that way." But Kelsey had already walked away.

CHAPTER EIGHTEEN

Beth was spending more time on campus. She was working with tutors and feeling good about how things were going. Her grades were solid Bs which made her happy. Everything was right in her world.

She dropped Mama off at the day care every morning and picked her up in the afternoon. Mama was participating and interacting and doing very well, the day care people told her. She'd had a couple more accidents so on the way home from school, Beth stopped to pick up some adult diapers.

She wandered through the store, unsure of where to look. She was in the health care department when she heard a voice that made her heart clench.

"Fancy meeting you here," Evelyn said.

"I heard you were in town." Beth kept her voice cool.

"And yet, you haven't reached out."

"Why would I?"

"Beth, listen. If I could take back what happened—"

"But you can't. See? That's the thing. You did what you did and no matter how many times you text me, it doesn't change that you used me and took calculated advantage of me."

"I didn't though. I was a fool to let you see that folder. I admit that. I own that. I beat myself up over that every day and every night."

"Sounds like a personal problem," said Beth.

"Give me another chance? I'm begging you."

"What? You're back in town so you need a townie to feed your ego? Find someone else this go around."

She spotted the diapers, grabbed two packs, and headed to the register. She was shaking as she walked out to her car. Evelyn Bremer was the last person she thought she'd see at the local store. She needed to pay better attention. She needed to look for that damned Mercedes in every parking lot everywhere in town.

Mama had had a bad day at day care. She'd been agitated and disruptive. The head of the center, Karen Colston, pulled Beth aside when she got there.

"We're concerned about your mother," Karen said.

"How so?"

"If this behavior continues, we won't be able to have her here. Surely you understand."

"But I thought you people were trained for this," said Beth.

"We are. And we can attempt to deescalate. But your mom wanted nothing to do with that."

"I'm sure it was a one-off."

"I hope so," said Karen.

Beth glanced over at Mama on the way home.

"How was your day today?"

"It was fine. I had fun."

"Did you?"

"Mm-hm."

"Good, Mama. That's great to hear."

Back at the house, Beth got Mama situated in the living room to watch her shows.

"You know, Mama, I was thinking."

"Yes, dear?"

"I got you some special underwear I want you to try for me."

"Special underwear? Why?"

"It should help in case you have an accident," said Beth.

"Accident? I don't have accidents. And I don't need special underwear. Now, let me watch my show."

Beth sat at the coffee table and worked on her homework until Kelsey announced that dinner was ready.

"I'm not hungry," Mama said. "I'm going to bed."

"But Kelsey made you a really good dinner."

"I'm going to bed."

"Do you need help?"

"Of course not."

Beth joined Kelsey in the dining room.

"How was her day?" Kelsey said.

"Not good. And now she's being obstinate. I'm going to call Dr. Hughes in the morning. I think it's time to get her checked out. Maybe there's some medication she can take."

"Beth, there's no magic pill. She's not going to get better."

"But maybe there's something to keep her from being so crotchety."

"Good luck with that."

They ate for a while in silence before Kelsey spoke up again.

"Are you going to try to see Evie while she's in town?"

"I ran into her today."

"Oh, good."

"Not really," Beth said. "She's a lying, conniving, underhanded bitch."

"Why do you say that? She did right by us with the farm, didn't she?"

"Yeah. She did. And now my appetite is gone. I'm going to go to my room and study."

"Look, whatever happened, I'm sure it was a misunderstanding," said Kelsey.

"Nope. It wasn't."

Beth took her plate to the kitchen then went to her room. She was struggling with a Creative Writing assignment when her phone buzzed. Evelyn. Shit.

I'm coming over tomorrow. I want to see Mama.

She's in day care.

I'll be over around five. See you then.

Shit. She was sure Kelsey had put Evelyn up to this. She stormed down the hall to where Kelsey was washing dishes.

"You think you're pretty smart, don't you?"

"How so?"

"Did you invite Evelyn here?"

"No." Kelsey stared at Beth, her expression unreadable.

"Bullshit. I don't want her here. I don't want her near Mama."

"You're so fucking selfish. Mama loves Evie. And Evie loves Mama. She wants to come visit? Then let her."

Beth spun and stormed out of the room. It was a conspiracy. And she'd be damned if she'd let them win.

She took a deep breath. Mama did love Evelyn. It wouldn't hurt for her to come visit. Beth would just make sure to stay in her room the whole time. Nothing said she had to interact with Evelyn. So, she wouldn't. Winning.

The next afternoon at four forty-five, Kelsey knocked on Beth's door. Beth was in the middle of math homework so barely acknowledged her.

"Hm?"

"I've got to run an errand. Mama's watching TV. You be okay for a few minutes?"

"Sure."

Beth knew Mama would be okay, so she stayed focused on her work. She almost jumped out of her skin at the sound of the doorbell a few minutes later.

"I got it," she called to Mama.

She opened the door and there stood Evelyn. She was wearing black skinny jeans and an orange golf shirt. She looked amazing. It took Beth a moment to get herself together.

"Oh," she said. "It's you."

"I told you I was coming. Now invite me in."

"Do I have to?"

"Yes." Evelyn laughed. As if this was some colossal joke. As if she hadn't ripped Beth's heart out just a few short months ago.

"Fine. I'll take you to Mama."

"Beth, we need to talk."

"No. We do not. I'll let you visit with Mama though. I'll be in my room studying. No interaction between us needed."

Evie followed Beth to where Mama sat in her easy chair. She didn't look good. She looked old and tired. Damn. But Evie forced a smile.

"Hi, Mama. Do you remember me?"

Mama's face lit up.

"You're my friend."

"I am, yes. My name is Evie. How are you?"

"I'm okay. I can't remember anything anymore, but I'm fine."

"Am I interrupting your TV time?" Evie said.

"Not at all. Are we going to feed the ducks?"

"Would you like to?"

"I'm kind of tired today. Can we go tomorrow?"

"Sure. Anything for you."

Evie noticed a puzzle on a folding table nearby.

"Would you like to work on a puzzle with me?" she said.

"Yes, please. If you could bring the table over here."

Evie got Mama sitting upright in her chair and brought the table over. She tried to think of something to say, but Mama seemed content to work the puzzle.

"You're not working with me," Mama said.

Evie could do the puzzle in her sleep. It was for children, obviously. And she didn't want to make Mama feel stupid.

"I'm sorry. I was enjoying watching you."

"I'd prefer if you helped."

"Okay. I'll help."

Evie moved some pieces around and helped Mama when she got frustrated.

"I need to use the bathroom," Mama said.

Evie helped her get up and go to her walker. Mama walked through the dining room and was in the kitchen when she cried out.

"Damn it."

Evie was at her side in a flash. She didn't need to ask what was wrong. Mama had made a mess all over herself and the kitchen floor.

"Stay here," Evie said gently. "I'll be right back."

She went into the bathroom and came back with several washcloths and some towels.

"We'll get you all cleaned up," she said.

Evie Bremer was not caregiver material. She wanted to go get Beth. To tell her what had happened, and to let Beth deal with it. She fought her overwhelming gag reflex and got Mama out of her dirty clothes and all cleaned up. She was wiping up the floor when Beth came out.

"You're still here? What are you doing?"

"She had an accident."

"Where is she?"

"I think she went to her room to get dressed."

Beth took off down the hall without so much as a thank you. Evie followed her, ready to give her a piece of her mind. She stopped in the doorway to Mama's room.

"Are you okay, Mama?" Beth said.

"I don't know why I do that."

"It's the disease, Mama."

"I don't want the disease. I want to get better. Please help me get better."

Evie's eyes burned. There was liquid in them that she wasn't used to. She blinked the tears away.

"I bought you some special underwear," Beth said. She handed one to Mama.

"These don't look like my underwear."

"They're not. But they'll help with the accidents. Please try one on?"

As Evie looked on, Beth carefully and gently helped her mom put on an adult diaper. Beth loved Mama so much. It was apparent. Why couldn't she care for Evie again like that?

The thought was unwelcome and made her eyes sting again. What kind of game was Evie playing? It wasn't a game. She wanted Beth and needed to figure out how to get her back.

"I don't like these," Mama said. "They're not comfortable."

"Please wear them for a while. Maybe through the night?"

"I'll try. But I don't think I like them."

"I understand," said Beth.

Evie went back to the kitchen to get the soiled garments and started a load of wash. Clearly her attempt at getting Beth to care for her again had backfired. All she'd managed to do was fall harder for Beth. If that was possible.

Beth and Mama were back in the kitchen.

"Thanks for cleaning that up. You could have come to get me."

"I thought about it. Believe me." Evie laughed. "But I handled it."

"Well, I appreciate it."

"Your mom asked if we could feed the ducks tomorrow. Would that be okay with you?"

"Sure. She'd really enjoy that."

"You're welcome to come along," said Evie.

"No, thanks. I'll be studying."

"Beth, come to Charlie's with me this evening. Just to talk, okay? Nothing else, I promise."

"I know nothing else. That's never going to happen again. But if you want to talk, I can be there at eight."

"I'll be there. And, thank you, Beth."

"Don't thank me yet," Beth said. "I don't have anything to say to you."

"Then you can just listen."

"Whatever."

"I should get going," said Evie. To Mama, she said, "Thanks for working the puzzle with me."

"You're not very good at puzzles," Mama said.

"No." Evie laughed. "I don't suppose I am."

"We can feed the ducks tomorrow?"

"Sure. I'll come by earlier tomorrow, if that's okay?" Evie looked at Beth, who shrugged.

"I pick her up from day care around four," Beth said.

"Maybe I could pick her up?"

"I could arrange that."

"Thanks, Beth."

"Whatever."

Evie drove back to her house in silence. No radio, no podcast, no music. She was going to have a drink with Beth in a little bit and she needed to prep herself. She'd beg if she had to, but one way or another, she had to get Beth back.

Chapter Nineteen

At eight fifteen, Beth pulled into Catfish Charlie's. She was intentionally late and hoped Evelyn hadn't waited for her. But no, she saw the Mercedes and knew Evelyn was still there. She didn't know why the hell she'd agreed to meet, but she was there so might as well go in.

She waited for her eyes to adjust to the darkness then looked around. She didn't see Evelyn anywhere. Odd. Maybe she'd just have a beer and leave. That would be wonderful.

"Hey there, Little Miss Richards," said Charlie. "Long time no see."

"It's been a bit. That's for sure."

"Coors Light?"

"Yes, please."

"Coming right up."

She sat at the bar and checked out the mirror. No Evelyn. This was her lucky night. She took a sip of beer. It felt good going down.

"I got us a booth," Evelyn said.

"What? You're here?"

"I said I would be. Now, will you join me?"

Charlie winked at Beth, who wasn't in the mood. She picked up her beer and got off her stool.

"Which booth?" she said.

"The one in the corner. Come on."

Beth followed Evelyn, every nerve on alert for some sort of sabotage. She didn't trust Evelyn for obvious reasons. She saw no reason to start now.

She sat across from Evelyn.

"What do you want?"

"First, I'd like you to turn the permafrost off."

"No can do, Evelyn. Look, you wanted to talk, so talk."

"Please, call me Evie."

"No Evelyn. Never again."

"What can I do to gain your forgiveness?"

"You can't," said Beth. "Look, you knew my history. You knew how new I was to this…to everything. You could have told me at any point it was just a game for you. But, no. You led me on and used months of studying me to try to get me to bed. How does any of that sound like grounds for forgiveness?"

"It wasn't a game for me, Beth."

"Spare me."

"I had feelings for you. I still do, if you must know."

"Translation," said Beth, "you were hot and bothered and had some fun. Now that you're back, you're bored and looking for more fun. You're not going to get it from me."

"It wasn't just fun and games."

"Right."

Evelyn took a deep breath and slowly exhaled.

"Okay. Not to change the subject, but I'm worried about your mom."

"Aren't we all?"

"How can I help?" Evelyn said.

"Why do you want to? It's certainly not because you care. I know you're incapable of that."

"I do care. Very much. Too much, obviously."

"Whatever," said Beth.

"You're okay with me picking her up from day care and taking her to feed the ducks?"

"I said I was, didn't I?"

"Beth, please. I can't take this cold shoulder."

"Then maybe I should leave." She drained what was left of her beer.

"No! Please don't. I'll buy you another beer."

"Suit yourself."

Beth took a sip of the beer Evelyn bought.

"How is it?" said Evelyn.

"Tastes fake. Phony. I guess it's because you bought it."

They sat in silence. Every muscle in Beth's body was tight, sore. She was on guard for any trick Evelyn might pull and it was getting painful. But she couldn't relax. That would lead to a different kind of pain. One she didn't want to experience again.

"I'll be leaving town again soon," said Evelyn.

"Good."

"But then I'll be back. Beth, please. Tell me what I can do to get you back."

"You can't. What part do you not understand? I opened up to you. I opened part of myself that had been closed my whole life. And it meant nothing to you. What the hell makes you think I want to go through that again?"

"It meant everything to me."

"It didn't. You had a whole fuckin' playbook on how to get me and you used it to manipulate me into believing you cared. I still can't believe I fell for that."

"I didn't follow a playbook. I followed my heart. Which you so callously broke and for some reason refuse to mend for me. I would have given anything to make us work, Beth."

"That is such utter bullshit," said Beth.

"Did I try to text you, Beth?"

"Yes. To save face. No other reason."

Evelyn lowered her voice.

"What can I do to prove my feelings for you?"

"You can quit doing that. I'm never going to buy into your bullshit again. What part of that don't you get?"

"Beth, you're killing me."

Beth looked up and saw tears in Evelyn's eyes. Her stomach quivered. Damn, did Evelyn really care about her? Her heart raced and her face warmed. Then she remembered who she was dealing with.

"Ha. You're funny. Make yourself cry. See if I care."

"I'm leaving. We're not getting anywhere. I'll see you tomorrow," said Evelyn.

Beth finished her beer and walked out into the crisp, autumn night. As she walked to her car, she passed the Mercedes. Evelyn was bent over the steering wheel, shoulders shaking. Was she laughing or crying? Beth told herself she didn't care.

Evie was a mess. This pain in her heart was something so unfamiliar to her. She needed to figure out a way to make it go away. But she knew only Beth could do that.

Evie sat up, wiped her eyes, and started her car. She drove back to her place and turned on some soft jazz. She sipped some Cabernet Sauvignon and let her mind drift back to happier times. Had it really only been a couple of months since she and Beth had sat on the floor of Beth's new house? Had it really been such a short while since their first kiss? And their last? She needed to taste Beth's lips again. But, how? When? Oh, God. This trip down memory lane was killing her. She needed to get some sleep. To escape her thoughts and feelings. She took a bath and climbed into bed. But it was a long time before she fell asleep.

She awoke to a ringing phone late the next morning.

"Hello?" she said.

"Evie? Did I wake you?"

"Sorry, Robert. Late night."

"With lovergirl?"

"What do you want?"

"When are you coming home?"

"In a couple of days," she said. "The stabilizing units are almost all in and then I'll come home until the windmills are ready to put up."

"Okay. I was just checking. I have this fear you're going to end up moving there."

"That will never happen. You have my word."

"Every so often, I've got to check in to be sure."

"I'll be home soon."

"Have fun, Evie."

"Yeah, right."

As she waited for her coffee to brew, she thought back to Charlie's with Beth. The place had been dark, which only made Beth's blue eyes stand out more. Those soft, expressive eyes that were rock hard last night. Evie wanted to cry again. But she couldn't. She had to get out to the farm to make sure things were going to plan.

She checked on the foundations. The last one was being poured. They were right on schedule. She talked to the foreman who affirmed they would be ready for the turbines in the next couple of weeks.

This news excited Evie. She loved to see an idea on paper come to life. The wind was howling out at the farm and she knew they'd be generating healthy energy in another month or so. She couldn't wait.

Evie checked her watch. She should go pick up Mama and take her to the lake. As she headed back to Vernon, she was feeling light on her toes. Everything was going smoothly. Well, everything except Beth.

She knew she should simply accept defeat where Beth was concerned, but she couldn't. First of all, it wasn't in her nature. Secondly, Beth had taken up residence in Evie's heart. And her heart had only been occupied once before. That had ended in disaster. She refused to let this relationship not work out.

The day care was a nice place. The patients, if that's what they were called, were sitting around a table drawing. Evie walked up to Mama after checking in at the front desk.

"Hi. Remember me?" she said. Mama looked at her with a blank expression. "I'm your friend. I'm taking you to feed the ducks."

Mama's face lit up.

"You are?"

"Are you ready?"

Mama nodded.

Evie got Mama's walker and walked slowly behind her as they got to the door. She waited until it was unlocked, then she guided Mama to her car.

"Do you remember this car?" Evie said.

"No."

"That's okay. We're going to have so much fun."

It was chilly at the lake and Evie was glad she'd thought to bring a blanket. Mama was skin and bones and would surely have frozen without being wrapped up.

Evie got them situated on a bench at the water's edge and Mama started tossing seeds into the lake. A whole flock of ducks came over and Mama squealed with childlike delight.

Evie sat next to her, keeping the blanket around her.

"Thank you," Mama said. "I love feeding ducks."

"You're quite welcome. I'd like to bring you out here often, if that's okay with you?"

"Oh, yes."

"Great."

Mama had a handful of seeds, but instead of tossing them, she dropped them at her feet.

"Mama?" Evie hoped she was okay.

Mama toppled forward along the shore.

"Mama?!" There was no response.

Evie called 9-1-1 before calling Beth.

"What?" Beth answered.

"Mama. Something's wrong. She's unconscious. I've called the ambulance. Meet me at the hospital." She disconnected and pulled Mama back a little. Evie hadn't realized her hair was in the water.

The ambulance arrived and sped off with Mama. Evelyn followed close behind. Her phone kept ringing, but she ignored it. The only thing that mattered was Mama. God, she hoped she'd be okay.

Beth pulled in right after Evie. They hurried into the emergency room.

"Thanks for all the info." Sarcasm dripped from Beth's words.

"I told you all I knew. Did you call Kelsey?"

"Of course." They approached the nurses' station. "My mama was just brought in. Mrs. Ida Richards?"

"They've taken her for surgery. I'm afraid I can't let you go to the waiting room without masks."

Evie fished through her purse and put hers on. Beth soon had hers on and Kelsey was wearing hers when she walked through the door.

"What's going on?" she said.

"Your guess is as good as mine." Beth glared at Evie.

"She just collapsed. She just toppled forward off the bench."

"And where were you?"

"I was sitting next to her. It happened so fast."

"I'm sure," said Kelsey.

"Come on, Kels," said Beth. "We should go up to the waiting room."

"Like it or not, I'm coming with," said Evie.

They sat in silence in the waiting room. They were the only ones there, which Evie found odd, but then reasoned that daily operations in Dallas probably outnumbered those in Vernon by a hundred fold.

The hours dragged on and Evie searched for something to say. Anything, to end the torturous silence. But she had nothing.

Finally, a woman in scrubs came into the waiting room.

"Ida Richards?" she said.

"Yes." Beth stood. "I'm her daughter. How is she?"

"She's not out of the woods yet. She had a stroke. There was a lot of bleeding on her brain. We got all the spots stopped, but we need to keep a close eye on her these next few days."

"Bleeding on her brain?" Beth glared at Evie. "Would that have happened when she hit her head at the lake?"

The doctor shook her head.

"No. As a matter of fact, whoever was with her at the lake probably saved her life with their quick actions."

"When can we visit her?" said Kelsey.

"She won't be able to have visitors for several hours. And then, one at a time for no more than five minutes. She's going to be very confused and very tired so don't let that alarm you."

"Understood," said Beth. "Thank you."

"Now, you all should get some food. It's likely going to be a long night. We'll keep you posted."

She disappeared behind the swinging doors. Evie sat with her hands in her face. Yes, she'd saved Mama's life, but what kind of life would Mama have now?

CHAPTER TWENTY

"Come on," Evie said. "I'm buying."

"What?" said Beth.

"You heard the doctor. We need to get something to eat. We need to keep our strength up. It's going to be a long night," said Kelsey.

"Right. Come on, Beth. Bury the hatchet just for tonight and let me buy dinner."

"I'm not hungry," she said.

"Then have a drink. Let's go to Charlie's," Kelsey said.

"Someone should be here in case Mama wakes up," Beth said.

"She's not going to be alert for hours. Beth, don't be an idiot. Come with us. It's on Evie's dime."

Beth finally agreed to go, but Evie could tell Beth would rather be having a root canal than allowing her to buy her drinks.

They stepped into Charlie's and as they stood waiting for their eyes to adjust, Beth's stomach let out a loud growl.

"Not hungry?" said Evie.

"Whatever. I suppose I could eat."

They were seated in the dining room and were looking over their menus.

"Is there anyplace in town that serves non-fried food?" Evie said.

"I'm sure there are but I'd never go there." Kelsey laughed.

"I'm getting a burger. That's not fried," said Beth.

"True. I guess that's what I'll get too."

They placed their orders then Evie and Kelsey split a bottle of wine while Beth took a long pull off her beer. Evelyn watched Beth's lips wrap around the bottle and thought of them sucking on any number of body parts. Her lips were so soft and tasted so good. Evie reined in her thoughts and raised her glass.

"To a full recovery for Mama," she said.

"Hear, hear," said Kelsey.

Beth didn't say a word but raised her bottle.

"I don't know that we've said thank you," said Kelsey. "For saving Mama's life."

Evie looked at Beth, who was peeling the label off her bottle.

"It's nothing. I simply called 9-1-1. What else could I have done?"

"You could have been sitting with her. You could have not left her alone to tumble to the ground." Beth sneered.

"I was sitting with her, Beth." Evie kept her voice soft. "I was sitting with her but she just toppled. I reached out to stop her, but she was already on the ground."

"How do we know you didn't push her? Maybe her head hitting the ground caused the stroke."

"Beth!" Kelsey looked ready to slap her. "How dare you? Evelyn has been nothing but kind and loving to Mama and our family. Don't you dare make such wild accusations."

"But we don't know," Beth continued. "We weren't there."

"That's right. We weren't. When was the last time you took Mama to feed the ducks? She loves doing that, but we don't take her. But Evie did. She and Mama were on an outing and Mama had a stroke. Now just accept that."

Beth sat silently and Evie wished there was some way to reach through her anger and aloof attitude and touch the warm, caring woman she'd discovered on her last trip. She was sure that Beth was still there. Evie just had no idea how to reach her.

Dinner was served and they ate in silence. Evie was worried about Mama and Beth and she assumed the sisters were worried about their mom. When the waitress came around to clear their plates, Evie asked to see the dessert menu. Beth and Kelsey groaned, but they didn't complain about sharing the huge piece of chocolate cake Evie got.

When she could come up with no other reason to keep them away from the hospital, she stood.

"We should probably get back," she said.

"Yeah. I hope nothing happened while we were away," Beth said.

"They would have let us know," said Kelsey. "They have your number."

Back in the waiting room, which they had to themselves, Evie decided to have some fun. If they were going to be sitting there for hours, they should have some fun.

"Kelsey," she said. "Tell me about your first kiss."

"What about it?"

"How old were you? Where was it?"

"I was fourteen. A freshman in high school. He was sixteen. And we kissed behind the stacks in the library."

"Tongue?" Evie said.

"Oh yeah." Kelsey grinned.

"Are we going to play Truth or Dare or something equally as juvenile now?" said Beth.

"Come on. It's fun. Who was your first kiss, Beth?" Kelsey said.

"None of your fuckin' business." She glared at Evie.

"Aw, come on. Was it Johnny Wilbur? David Benson?"

"Never mind," said Evie. "Beth's right. It was a juvenile question. And I apologize."

"Jeez," said Kelsey. "You two seriously need to get a room to clear the air or something. The tension between you two is overwhelming."

"Mind your own fuckin' business," said Beth. She moved to a chair across the room from Kelsey and Evie.

"Go talk to her," Kelsey said. "Please?"

"She won't talk to me. I'd love it if she would, but she won't."

"Try?"

Evie crossed the room to where Beth was sitting. Beth stood.

"Are you going to fight me?" said Evie.

"No. I'm just moving."

Evie grabbed Beth's arm.

"Beth, we need to talk."

"No, we don't. See, I've got nothing to say to you and I know better than to believe anything that comes out of your mouth. So there's no point in talking."

But Beth's body betrayed her. The feel of Evelyn's hand on her arm sent tingles across her body. Her arm felt on fire where Evie had touched her. Damn it.

Evelyn dropped her hand and Beth immediately missed it. She missed the softness, the warmth, the contact. But she didn't want contact with Evelyn, she reminded herself. Evelyn was the last person she'd ever want anything from again.

The nurse stepped through the doors.

"Mrs. Richards?"

"Yes."

"She's ready to see you. One person at a time. Who wants to go first?"

"You go, Beth," Evelyn said.

"Okay."

Beth stared down at the tiny, frail body in the hospital bed. When had her mama shrunk so? She remembered Mama standing five six growing up. Now Beth would be surprised if she broke five foot.

She had tubes and IVs plugged into her and she was surrounded by machines. It was surreal and Beth fought hard not to cry.

"Mama?"

Mama opened her eyes and looked at Beth. Her eyes showed fear, terror even.

"Who are you?" said Mama. "Where am I? Where are my children? They need to take me home."

She sounded frantic and the machines started beeping horrendously.

"Calm down, Mama."

"No. I need to see Beth."

She sat up and more machines beeped. A nurse came in and eased her down on her back.

"You're going to have to leave," the nurse said. "You're upsetting her."

"But—"

"No buts. Your sister can come in if you like, but if Mrs. Richards continues to be upset, we'll have to stop visitors for the night."

Beth was deflated as she walked down the hall and back to the waiting room.

"How is she?" Kelsey stood to greet Beth.

"Not good." Beth shook her head. "She's really confused and really upset. She didn't know who I was. Got all freaked out. A nurse had to come in and calm her down. You can try though. Maybe you'll have better luck."

Kelsey swallowed hard and nodded.

"I'll give it my best shot."

Beth sat in the chair Kelsey had vacated.

"I'm sorry Mama reacted that way," said Evelyn.

Beth shrugged.

"What do you expect? She has Alzheimer's. Waking up in a strange place has got to be the most frightening experience in the world."

"I'm sure you're right. How did she look?"

"Tiny. I don't know. She looked like a kid in an oversized bed."

Evelyn squeezed Beth's hand.

"I can't imagine how hard this is for you."

Beth, lost in thoughts about Mama, took a minute to realize she was actually getting comfort from Evelyn. When she realized, she pulled her hand away.

"Beth, please."

"No."

Before the tension could escalate, Kelsey was back.

"How'd it go?" said Beth.

"Terrible." She broke into tears. Evelyn held her while she cried. Beth looked on, wishing Evelyn had never shown her face back in Vernon.

Mama didn't need her. Kelsey didn't need her. They could take care of their own. And God knows, Beth didn't need her.

"You should try," Kelsey said. "Maybe Mama will talk to you."

"No," said Evelyn. "I'm not even going to try. I'll swing by tomorrow and check on her."

"That won't be necessary," Beth said. "We're perfectly capable of taking care of Mama."

"I'm not saying you aren't. I just happen to be very fond of your mama whether you like it or not. So I will be visiting."

"That would be great. Beth, where are your manners? You've been treating Evie like shit and I don't appreciate it."

"Whatever."

"No. Not whatever. Both of you sit down and we'll talk it through until you can be civil to her."

"Not going to happen," said Beth. "Now, come on, Kelsey. Let's get home."

"I'll get a ride with Evie. Thanks anyway."

"Suit your fuckin' self."

She got home and tried to study but was too upset. Upset at Evelyn for her very existence and upset at Kelsey for taking Evelyn's side. Maybe Beth should come clean to Kelsey so she'd understand what a snake Evelyn was. But no. Beth wasn't about to admit how hard she'd fallen and the pain it had caused. She'd never admit to Kelsey her involvement with Evelyn. It was a secret she'd take to the grave.

Morning came early. Too early. Beth hurried to shower and get ready so she could meet her tutor at eight. She hadn't finished the assignment her math tutor had given her the day before so she was sure she'd get a lecture. One she was not in the mood for.

She got through tutoring by playing the sympathy card. Andrew, her tutor, understood why Beth hadn't completed her assignment and they spent the hour they had working the problems together. Beth had really improved and was feeling good about herself, really good, for the first time since the whole Evelyn debacle.

"You're really getting the hang of this," said Andrew. "Keep up the good work."

He gave her another assignment and she started classes for the day. Things were making sense, to a degree. She was exhausted and having a hard time concentrating.

When classes were done for the day, she drove to the hospital to check on Mama. She found Kelsey in the waiting room.

"What are you doing here? Why aren't you in with Mama?"

Kelsey looked at her with swollen, red-rimmed eyes.

"She didn't know me again. Evie is with her now."

"Great. So I've got to wait for a stranger to finish visiting before I get to see my own Mama."

"She's not a stranger, Beth. I'm sure she'll be out soon."

"I don't know what you see in her. She's a manipulative bitch. And you're under her spell."

"I'd venture to say you're under her spell, too, or you wouldn't fight so hard to prove you're not."

"I'm not under anyone's spell," said Beth. She was fuming. How could Kelsey not see through Evelyn's persona?

Evelyn came out to the waiting room.

"How is she?" said Kelsey.

"She's okay. Go on back, Beth. She's in a pretty good mood."

Beth hurried back to find Mama laying there, eyes wide.

"Mama? What's up?"

"I can't feel my right side. Help me. Please help me."

Beth pushed the button to call a nurse but decided she'd better go find one. She got to the nurses' station.

"My mama can't feel her right side. Help."

The nurse said to another nurse, "Call the doctor. STAT."

Beth followed her as she ran down the hall. Mama was unconscious. Try as they might they were unable to wake her.

"You need to leave," the nurse told Beth. "Now."

Beth once again fought tears as she made her way back to the waiting room.

"What's wrong, Beth?" said Evelyn.

"I don't know. But I think she's having another stroke."

Chapter Twenty-one

Shit." Kelsey stepped into Beth's arms and sobbed.

"She was fine when I left her," said Evie. "Why do you think she had another stroke?"

"She said she couldn't feel her right side. Then she was completely unresponsive by the time the nurse and I got back to her room."

"I'm so sorry." And Evie meant it. She didn't know how many strokes Mama's fragile body and mind would be able to withstand.

Kelsey stepped away from Beth as the nurse approached.

"It appears your mom has had another stroke," she said. "She's back in surgery. It could be a few hours. If you wanted to step away for a few."

"I'm not going anywhere." Beth sat. "I'm waiting right here."

"Suit yourself. We'll come get you when she's out of the woods."

"Beth, you don't want to sit here alone stressing out. Come on. Let's get out of here."

"Not a chance. You didn't see her. She was terrified. I'm scared for her."

"Okay. I'll stay with you," said Evie. "Kelsey, you want to go on a food run or something?"

"I'm not hungry. I'll sit here, too."

Evie was disappointed. She wanted time alone with Beth. She was dying inside at the way Beth hated her and needed to do something to make it better. That wouldn't happen with Kelsey there.

They all got out their phones and sat in silence. Evie tried to be amused by what she saw on Facebook, but everything irritated her. Life went on for everybody while Mama's life hung in the balance.

She looked over at Kelsey who was scrolling mindlessly as well. Beth was staring out the window, phone apparently forgotten.

"Y'all sure you want to just sit here? It's only been a half hour and I'm going nutso."

"Then leave," Beth snapped. "No one is making you stay."

"Knock it off, Beth," said Kelsey. "I wouldn't feel right leaving. But if you need to, Evie, you can."

"I'm just here for moral support," Evie said. "If you two want to stay, I'll stay."

"Don't do me any favors," said Beth.

"I'm leaving," Kelsey said. "I'm going to pick up dinner. When I get back, I expect you two to be getting along again."

Before either of the other two could say anything, Kelsey disappeared down the hall.

"Shit," said Beth.

"It's actually okay," Evie said. "We need to clear the air."

"No. We don't. My mama is in surgery for her second stroke. That's all that matters to me. If you think anything you say or do is important right now, you're wrong."

"Please quit pushing me away, Beth."

"Did you not hear me?"

"I did. And you're right. But your mama loved the idea that you were happy when we were together. I think she'd be happy knowing we were trying again."

"Nice try," said Beth.

Evie sat in the chair next to Beth.

"Please? Can we please try again?" she said.

"Do you not have a new playbook to consult? Surely one of your researchers has told you how to trick me again."

"It's not like that. How can I convince you that file had nothing to do with us?"

"I know that it is like that. I read the file. Intimate details about my family's life and mine. You tricked me. Sorry it's so frustrating to think you can't trick me again."

"You know in your heart of hearts that that's not how it happened. I didn't trick you. I followed my feelings and you followed yours. I'm sorry you ever saw that damned file."

"Ya think? And now you think I should put my heart in the position to get crushed again? For fuck's sake, Evelyn, you were my first kiss. I was ready to do things with you I'd never done before."

Evie felt that comment to her core. She needed Beth. She wanted Beth. And it went beyond anything she'd ever felt before. She longed to be Beth's first lover. But how to get her there?

She took Beth's hand, but Beth pulled it away. She stood and walked over to the window and stared out at the darkness. Evie watched her, debating whether she should go to her. Common sense told her to stay put.

She crossed the waiting room and stood close to Beth. So close she could feel the heat radiating off her. They were a hair's breadth apart. When Beth didn't move away, Evie placed her hands on Beth's shoulders. Beth leaned back into her.

"Well, this looks promising," Kelsey said.

"It's not." Beth glared at Evie then walked over to help herself to some chicken strips.

Evie was a mess. Her whole body was on fire. Feeling Beth's body against her reignited a flame that had been smoldering for months. She needed her like she'd never needed anyone before. But how to gain her trust and pick things up where they'd left off?

She nibbled on a chicken strip and tried to calm her racing heart and hormones. Damn, she had it bad.

"You're not hungry?" Kelsey was watching her.

"I am. Just don't want to inhale. Sorry." She smiled. It was a weak smile and she knew it.

"Well, since we have nothing to do but wait, we're going to play a little game after we eat."

"That sounds good," said Evie.

"Good. We're going to play, 'What the hell happened between you two and why is it over now?'"

"Sounds like a stupid game," said Beth. "And one I'm sure as hell not going to play."

"You're acting like a lovesick teenager and have been for months. It's time to talk about it. Get it out in the open. We can dissect it and then we'll all be able to move on," said Kelsey.

"Shut the fuck up. You don't know what you're talking about so just let it go."

"Evie?" Kelsey turned to her. "What are your thoughts?"

"I'd love to talk about it. But I doubt Beth's ready."

"Thank God someone around here has a brain."

"Look, I have a brain, too," Kelsey said. "And I know something happened between you two. I can only surmise you were romantically involved and it didn't end well. So, talk to me. How did it end and how can we move past it?"

Beth had had it. She didn't want to talk about anything. Not with Evelyn and certainly not with Kelsey.

"I need to get some fresh air." She was walking down the hall when she heard the surgeon.

"Mrs. Richards?"

She ran back. Her heart dropped. Something in the surgeon's demeanor scared her.

"How is she? When can we see her?" Beth said.

"I'll be honest. It's touch-and-go right now. She didn't do well in surgery. Her heart stopped twice. We don't know if she's going to make it. I'm sorry to tell you that."

"But she might make it?" Kelsey said.

"It's possible. We're going to keep a close eye on her."

"When can we see her?" Beth said again.

"Not for a long time. We need to keep her sedated for a while. I'd suggest you go home and get some rest. Come back and check on her in the morning."

"Do you have my number?" said Beth.

"I'm sure we have all pertinent information. You would have filled that out when we admitted her."

"Can you call us when she wakes up?"

"Sure. But it won't be for some time. As I said, we're keeping a close eye on her."

"Fine. We'll be back early."

"Great."

"Thank you, Doctor," said Evelyn. "We appreciate all you've done."

He nodded solemnly, turned, and left.

"Shit," said Beth. "I'm going to Charlie's."

"Me, too," said Kelsey.

"I guess I am too. Since I'm riding with Kelsey."

The bar was empty on that weeknight. They got their drinks and sat in a booth. Beth on one side. Kelsey and Evelyn on the other.

"How are you two holding up?" Evelyn said.

"I'm not," said Beth.

"I'm holding out hope," said Kelsey. "What about you?"

"I'm gutted and she's not even my mom."

Beth looked up and saw the tears in Evelyn's eyes. She appreciated them. She understood completely but appreciated them as they showed Evelyn cared for Mama.

"She's going to pull through," said Kelsey. "She's a fighter."

"I hope you're right," Beth said. "God, I hope you're right."

"Damn. I just feel so useless. Like why can't we do something to fix this? I'm not used to just sitting around waiting for outcomes. I'm used to making them happen," Evelyn said.

"That's true. You're a mover and shaker," said Kelsey.

"I wonder if we could airlift her to Dallas. I'd make sure she had the best doctors."

"She's probably too fragile," Beth said. "But, thank you. I appreciate the thought."

And she meant it. Just because things hadn't worked out between the two of them didn't mean Evelyn didn't want the best for Mama. And Beth didn't doubt that Evelyn would make sure she got top of the line doctors instead of rural doctors in Vernon, Texas. Beth was embarrassed of where she lived. For the first time in her life, she wished she was from a big city, too.

"I'm sure our doctors know what they're doing," said Kelsey. "I'm sure they're giving her the best care there is."

"I hope you're right," Beth said. "Still. I think I'd be more comfortable if she was getting treated by some big city doctor."

"She's not big city. Mama would rather have her local doctors working on her. We've got to have faith."

"We do have to keep the faith. These are the doctors we have," said Evelyn. "So we have to believe they know what they're doing."

Last call came and they grabbed three more drinks.

"No news is good news," Evelyn said.

"Exactly," said Kelsey.

They finished their drinks and stood in the cool night in front of the bar.

"You staying with us?" Beth said. "Or is Kelsey dropping you off at your place?"

"Would it be okay if I stayed with y'all? So I don't miss anything?"

"That would be great," Kelsey said.

Beth lay awake fighting tears, trying not to go over worst-case scenarios. But she was scared. So fucking scared. The door to the bedroom opened.

"Beth?"

"Evelyn?"

"Will you hold me, please? I'm scared and don't want to be alone."

Every muscle in Beth's body tightened and she thought for sure she'd tell Evelyn where to go.

"Come on in," she heard herself say.

Evelyn backed into Beth's arms.

"Thank you, Beth. I needed this."

"Sh. You try to go to sleep now."

Beth's senses were reeling. She was worried about Mama, but having Evelyn in her arms felt so right. And it was good. She needed something good in her life. She wondered if she'd been fighting too hard. Maybe she could give Evie another shot. Maybe she could keep her heart out of it this time.

The shrill sound of the phone woke Beth out of a deep sleep. She checked the time. Four seventeen. What the hell?

"Hello?"

"Is this Beth Richards?"

"It is."

"Miss Richards, this is Dr. Mouton. I'm sorry to have to tell you, but your mom didn't make it."

"What? Is this some kind of a joke?"

"I'm really sorry. You can come see her before we take her away."

"We'll be right there."

She threw her phone across the room. Angry tears streamed down her cheeks. She'd failed her mama. She hadn't been able to save the woman who had always been there for her.

"Beth?" She'd forgotten about Evie.

"She didn't make it."

"Oh, Beth. I'm so sorry. Come here."

Beth allowed Evie to wrap her in her arms as she sobbed. Ugly, ferocious sobs tore her body and she let them out. She let them all out.

When she'd cried enough for the time being, Beth pulled away.

"We have to go see her. Before they take her away. I'd better go tell Kelsey."

"I'm right here," Kelsey said. "I heard the phone."

She crossed the room and sat on the bed.

"Shit," said Beth. "Fucking shit. This sucks."

"We need to get dressed and get over there." How was Evie so calm? "I'll drive since I don't think either of you are capable right now. Let's meet in the kitchen in five minutes."

CHAPTER TWENTY-TWO

The next couple of days passed in a blur for Beth. Neighbors from Walker came by with casseroles and other meals she couldn't imagine eating. Evie was staying at the house and managing visitors and the like.

But it had been up to Beth and Kelsey to write the obituary, make the final arrangements, and prepare to say their final goodbyes. Beth tried to remember everything Mama had wanted, but her mind was mush. She only hoped she was getting everything right.

The day of the memorial service arrived. It was a cool, crisp November morning. The church in Vernon was packed to overflowing. Everyone had loved Mama. This was apparent.

Beth, Kelsey, and Evie sat in the front row. Evie turned around and looked at the church.

"I didn't know there were this many people in this town," she said.

"There are people here I haven't thought about in years," Kelsey said.

"Beth?" said Evie. "Do you want to look at the crowd?"

"No. I just want to get through this."

Evie reached across Kelsey and squeezed Beth's hand.

"I'm here for you."

"I appreciate that."

They stood as the pastor made his way to the altar. He droned on about how special Mama had been and how certain he was that she was with Papa in heaven. He talked about living a good, clean life like Mama to get to the promised land.

It was time for the eulogies. The church was silent, and it took Beth a minute to realize she was supposed to say a few words. Everyone was waiting on her.

"I don't think I can do this," she said.

"You want Kelsey to go instead?" Evie said.

"No. It's my duty. Give me a sec."

Beth stepped up onto the altar and stood behind the podium. She looked out at the congregation looking back at her. *Say something, damn it. Start talking.*

"My mama was a special woman as any of you can attest to. She loved her family and friends like nobody's business." She took a deep, shaky breath and continued. "Her last few years on earth weren't easy and it sucked watching her suffer."

She saw Evie smile and realized what she'd said in a church. Oh well. Too late now.

"Alzheimer's is not a disease for the weak. It's not fair that she had it or that she had a stroke which claimed her life. None of it's fair. I know she's in heaven where she belongs. She was too good for this world anyway."

"You did good," Kelsey whispered as Beth sat again.

The tears flowed silently down Beth's cheeks. She wiped them away gruffly. She didn't have time for tears. She had a life she had to figure out how to live without her precious mama.

The reception was held at Beth's house, and she stood staunchly and accepted condolences from everyone.

"You need to eat," said Evie.

"I'm not hungry."

"I know. But I want you to sit down in the living room and eat a plate. I'll get it for you."

Beth sat in the living room, surrounded by people she didn't want to talk to. But she knew she had to be gracious. These people were hurting too. Evie brought her a plate with bread, salami, and cheeses.

"I can't eat all that."

"You need to try."

As she sat nibbling on the food, people streamed by, telling her how much they had loved her mom. It felt good to hear, but at the same time, she didn't want to hear it. She wanted these people gone. She wanted to let herself grieve. Finally. It was sinking in that Mama was not coming home from the hospital. That Beth would never hear her voice again. And it hurt. It hurt like hell.

"I see Evie made you eat too." Kelsey sat next to her.

"Yeah."

"You doin' okay?"

"No. You?"

"Not really. I don't know what we would have done without Evie these past few days."

"Yeah. She's been a godsend."

"She really has. I don't know what we're going to do when she leaves tomorrow."

"What?" Beth felt like she'd been punched in the gut. "What do you mean?"

"She's going back to Dallas. But she'll be back in a week or two."

"Shit," said Beth.

"Yeah."

More people streamed by to offer condolences, but Beth was only going through the motions. Her heart and mind reeled at the fact that Evie was leaving again. This didn't hurt as bad as the first time, but it was close.

She and Kelsey had become so reliant on her. In a different way than she'd relied on her in the past, but still. With Evie gone, how would Beth and Kelsey cope? Could they cope? She guessed she'd find out.

Evie stood in the hall looking into the living room. She was watching Beth closely. She kept an eye on Kelsey, too, but Beth was the one that worried her. Yes, she'd finally cried at the service, but it was short-lived. She needed to let it all out. Maybe tonight when everyone was gone, she'd be able to feel her feels. God, Evie hoped so.

Beth was a strong woman. There was no denying that. But she had her breaking point and she had to be reaching it. Evie wished she could tell everyone to clear out and leave the sisters in peace but it wasn't her place. Her place was to pick up after the guests and keep them fed.

She also wished she could hold Beth. Just hold her and let her cry. But she didn't know how comfortable Beth would be with that. Beth seemed to tolerate Evie's presence, but Evie still wasn't clear if Beth was glad she was there or not.

Kelsey spewed gratitude. Kelsey wasn't Beth. Yes, Evie cared deeply for Kelsey but she wasn't Beth. It was Beth's gratitude Evie craved. Hell, any positive emotion from Beth would be welcome.

And Evie hated that she had to leave the next day. But the windmills had been ready for a week, and it was time for her to get back to Dallas and make the arrangements to get the windmill farm up and running. She'd be back in a week or less and hoped to stay with the sisters when she was there. It was something she needed to broach to them. Fingers crossed.

Slowly but surely people finished paying their tributes and started making their way out of the house. Evie found Beth just where she'd left her.

"You okay?" Evie said.

"I'm numb."

"That's understandable. Why don't you go soak in the tub for a few? Just to decompress."

"I think I'll do that."

"Want me to scrub your back?" The words were out before she could stop them.

Beth stared hard at Evie. Evie wished she could tell what she was thinking.

"I'll be okay," Beth said finally. "Thanks though."

Evie cleaned the house while Beth bathed and Kelsey lay down for a bit. She got all the plates and cups thrown out and put the furniture back where it belonged. When she was through, she knocked on the bathroom door.

"You doing okay?"

"Yeah. I'll be out in a few."

"I'm off to buy beer and wine. I'll be right back."

"Sounds good."

Evie got back from the store and saw the bathroom door open. She checked in Beth's room but she wasn't there. She wandered down the hall and found Beth lying on Mama's bed. Evie crossed the room and gently rubbed Beth's back. She felt her shuddering and knew Beth had finally reached the point where she could grieve.

"I'll let you be," Evie whispered.

Beth rolled over and took her hand.

"No. Don't go. Lay with me."

Evie climbed into bed and spooned Beth. She wasn't used to being the spooner, but this wasn't a sexual experience. She was simply comforting a friend. A very special friend who hurt like hell.

"What's going on in here?" Evie rolled over to see Kelsey standing in the doorway. She motioned her to join them.

Kelsey climbed in front of Beth and the three of them lay like that for a very long time. Evie lost track of time as she held Beth and occasionally stroked Kelsey's hair.

Finally, Beth said, "Okay. That's enough. I need a beer."

"And I need tissue," laughed Kelsey.

"Yeah. That too."

Evie got up and opened a bottle of wine and took a Coors Light out of the fridge. She only had to wait a few minutes before Beth wandered into the dining room, face red and splotchy.

"You feel better?" Evie said.

"Marginally. It fucking hurts, ya know? Like, I'm never going to see Mama again. Ever."

"I know. And you two were so close."

Beth nodded as she took the beer Evie offered. She took a long pull off it then sat down at the dining room table.

"So what now?" said Evie.

"I don't know."

Kelsey entered the dining room and took the glass of wine Evie held up.

"Will anything ever feel normal again?" Kelsey said.

"It's going to take time," said Evie. "But you'll get there."

"I guess I need to get back to school," said Beth. "That'll help. I need to finish my degree."

"I never asked," said Evie. "What's your degree in?"

"Business management."

"Cool. Maybe you can get a job with my company."

"Yeah? That'd be cool."

"What about me? I'm not going to Dallas," Kelsey said.

"What about you?" Evie said. "You just want to get married and have babies. You could do that in Dallas."

"Vernon is more my speed," said Kelsey.

"Well, you don't have to take care of Mama anymore. You should find someplace, besides bars, to meet eligible bachelors."

"Where?"

"I don't know," admitted Beth.

"I guess I'll have to get a job now," Kelsey said.

"Maybe you could work at the place y'all used to take Mama," said Evie. "You'd be great there."

"That's an idea. But not right now. It's too soon."

"I get that."

"We should play cards or something," said Kelsey. "Something to take our minds off Mama."

"I'm game if you are." Evie looked at Beth, who shrugged.

"Sure. Why not?"

They played rummy until the wee hours of the morning. No one was feeling any pain by the time Evie said she had to get some sleep.

"I've got to drive home tomorrow," she said. "I hate to break up the party, but I really need to get some shut-eye."

"Yeah. Sleep would be a good thing," said Kelsey. "Let's turn in."

Evie waited until Kelsey was silent in her room. She went down the hall and knocked on Beth's door.

"Come in," Beth said.

Evie opened the door and found Beth sitting on the side of her bed.

"You can't sleep?" said Evie.

"Not yet. I will though." She patted the spot next to her on the bed. "What's up?"

"I just wanted to talk to you for a few. Make sure you understand that I have to leave but that I'll be back in a week or less."

"I understand."

"May I stay here when I come back?"

"Of course."

They sat together in silence with Evie wondering why she didn't leave. Why was she just sitting there? Yes, she was drunk and yes, she wanted Beth, but now was not the time or the place.

Beth surprised her by kissing her. Tenderly, gently at first, but then with pent up passion that matched Evie's. Soon Evie was on her back and Beth was on top of her, tongue probing the depths of her mouth.

Evie felt parts of her body come awake that had been dormant since Beth had written her off before. She struggled not to touch Beth's breasts or slide her hand inside her jeans.

She finally pushed Beth off her.

"Beth." She was breathless. "Now isn't the time."

"But I want you. I need you. I want to feel alive the way only you can make me feel."

"I appreciate that. And I want you too. But we've both had a lot to drink and you're still recovering from the loss of your mom. Hold that thought though, Beth. Because when I come back, we're going to take it to the limit."

"I'll hold you to that."

Chapter Twenty-three

Beth sat in her algebra class trying to concentrate. She'd been back in school a few days and the harder she tried, the more she thought about dropping out. She wondered if she could get a break for having her mama die. Like if they'd let her have the rest of the semester off and pick up where she left off next semester. But she only had a month left. Surely she could pull it together. Life just sucked.

Evie was back, too, which occupied a lot of Beth's mind. She was so appreciative of Evie for everything she did for her and Kelsey. Was that gratitude twisting things in Beth's brain? Did she really care for Evie again? Or was she just grateful? She didn't know. All she knew was she seemed to be biding her time, waiting for another chance to kiss Evie. She needed her in a bad way and couldn't wait to get Evie naked.

Of course, the thought also terrified Beth as she had no idea what to do once Evie was naked. She just knew she wanted the chance to figure it out.

She dragged her attention back to class. It was boring, but she fought to stay focused. It was her last class of the day and then she'd get to go home and see Evie. The thought had parts of her she seldom paid attention to twitching and throbbing.

Class finally ended and she scooped up her books and laptop and slid them in her backpack. She hoisted the backpack over a shoulder and started to the parking lot. She was almost to her car when she heard someone call her name. She turned to see Caleb, one of the other students, walking toward her.

"Hey, Caleb. What's up?"

"I was really lost in algebra today. I was wondering if we could grab a cup of coffee and you could explain it to me?"

Beth didn't have time to teach this young kid algebra. She wanted to get home to see Evie. But he looked so forlorn, she couldn't say no.

She reviewed the lesson with him and he finally caught on.

"Thanks for working with me," he said.

"You're welcome. Happy to help."

"Can we go out sometime?" he blurted.

"What? Like a date?"

"Yeah." He was crimson.

"Caleb, you seem like a really nice guy. But I'm old enough to be your mother."

"I don't care."

She smiled at him.

"I'm flattered. I really am. But, I'm taken." Was that a lie to put him off? Or did she really consider herself taken by Evie? They hadn't officially gotten back together. But, still…

"Oh, I'm sorry. I understand. Thanks again for the help."

They walked out to the parking lot.

"Good luck with everything, Caleb. I'll see you in class."

She drove home smiling. She was flattered that she'd been asked out, even by someone way too young for her. And the wrong gender. It was sweet nonetheless.

Beth walked in the front door and listened. The house sounded eerily quiet.

"Kelsey? Evie? Anyone home?"

There was no answer so Beth went to her room to work on her homework. She'd been at it a while. She lost track of time. She heard laughter and chatting and her stomach clenched. Evie was back.

She left her room and found Kelsey and Evie in the kitchen.

"What are you two up to?"

"Buying groceries to get ready for Thanksgiving," Evie said. "It's next week you know."

"Is it really?"

"Yes," said Kelsey. "You're off next week, right?"

"Huh? Yeah. I suppose I am. But isn't it too soon to buy the turkey?"

"Not if we freeze it," said Evie. "Now get out of our way and let us get things put away."

"I'll be in my room if you need me."

"Oh no you don't," said Evie. "You'll grab a beer and sit at the table. We're almost through and then we're going to play Trivial Pursuit. It's a day of celebration."

"What are we celebrating?"

"Thanksgiving!" Evie and Kelsey said together.

"It's officially the holidays. And we need a day to cheer ourselves up."

"Sounds good," said Beth. Their celebratory mood was infectious.

"How was school?" said Kelsey

"Interesting. Well, not school per se. But after school. I got asked out."

"You *what*?" Evie looked at her wide-eyed.

"I got asked out." Beth laughed. "A classmate asked me out."

"And are you going?" Kelsey glared at her.

"Are you kidding? He's like half my age. But it was flattering."

"You little shit." Evie ruffled her hair as she sat next to her with her glass of wine. "You had me scared."

"Am I not allowed to date?" Beth stared at Evie, wanting to hear her say no.

"It's a free country," Evie said.

"That's what I needed to hear."

"It is?"

"Look, you confuse me. You've got to know that."

"You dumped me."

"Whatever."

"That's enough, you two," said Kelsey. "Let's play a game and try to get along."

Evie wasn't much in the mood to play a game. She wanted, needed Beth to tell her she didn't want to date anyone but her. But obviously, that wasn't going to happen. Still, it wouldn't be fair to Kelsey to piss on her mood, so she settled in to beat them in the game.

The game lasted hours and there was much laughter and drinking. Beth and Evie had all their pies and were finally heading for the center. Kelsey still only had four pies, but she was valiantly trying to get her other two and win.

Beth ended up winning and did a victory lap around the table. Evie couldn't help but laugh. Beth was so stinkin' cute. And she was so proud of herself. Evie allowed her super competitive self to relax and be happy for Beth.

"I'm famished," Evie said. "It's eight o'clock and we haven't had dinner. Let's order in."

"Sounds good," said Kelsey. "What do we want?"

"More beer," said Beth.

"Did you finish that twelve-pack already?"

"No. I was just joking. I'll grab another beer while y'all decide on dinner."

"I know what we're having. Leave it to me," said Evie. She was working on her phone. She knew just what Beth would love and hoped Kelsey would love it, too.

Dinner arrived from Logan's Inn and Beth was duly impressed.

"Evie. You remembered?"

"There's not much about my time in Walker and Vernon that I'll forget."

"Before you two fall into bed, let's eat," said Kelsey.

Dinner was enjoyed by all. Evie was proud of herself for knowing just what to order. Beth's steak was cooked to perfection. As was Kelsey's and hers, but Beth was the one who mattered. Beth was all that mattered. How to convince her of that?

They got the table cleaned up and Kelsey yawned.

"Hate to break up the party, but I'm exhausted. I'll see y'all in the morning."

Evie said good night to Kelsey then sat in an uncomfortable silence with Beth.

"I should turn in, too," Beth said.

"Sleep well."

"Thanks. You, too."

Evie waited until Beth's room was quiet. Then she went in there.

"Beth? Can we talk?"

"What about?"

"You're not really that tired are you?"

"Not really. What do you need?"

Beth's voice was cool and aloof. But it didn't deter Evie. She took a deep breath as she sat on Beth's bed.

"Did that kid really ask you out today?"

"Sure did."

"I don't like that." There. She'd said it.

"Why not?"

"I hate the thought of you dating anyone other than me."

"I know that's not true. You used information on me to get me to fall for you so you could get the house. It wasn't real. I know that." But the words sounded worn out and the excuse was dated. She wanted to be with Evie so desperately. If only Evie felt the same.

"If you'll recall, oh stubborn one, I already had the house before I kissed you for the first time."

"What do you want from me? You want a little fling before you go back to Dallas? You want someone to warm your bed while you're here? Well, find someone else."

"I don't want anyone else. And I don't want a fling. I want something real. And I believe you do too."

"Not with yo—"

Evie didn't let her finish. She kissed Beth, softly, tenderly, trying to convey her feelings yet giving Beth an out.

Beth didn't seem to need an out. The next thing Evie knew, Beth's tongue was in her mouth, probing deep, roaming around. Evie ended up on her back with Beth on her, griding into her. Kissing her so hard she was sure their lips would bruise.

Evie ran her hands through Beth's hair and down her back and arms. Beth was so muscular. Her body was simultaneously hard and soft and Evie couldn't get enough.

Beth ended the kiss and nibbled down Evie's cheek. She sucked on her earlobe and Evie felt herself swelling at the sensations Beth was creating. Would tonight be the night? Would they finally consummate this thing they had?

The feel of Beth's tongue on her neck had Evie's nipples in pain. Never had she been so aroused and she'd been with plenty of women. This was different. Gone was the timid, unsure Beth. This new confident Beth had Evie aroused beyond words.

Beth kissed Evie's exposed chest and Evie longed for her to rip her shirt off and suck her nipples. She needed that. But Beth was in charge. Beth kissed her way back to Evie's mouth.

"Is that what you wanted?" Though her heavy breathing belied the cool tone of her voice.

"Oh, Beth. That and so much more."

"Now's not the time or place."

"Now's the perfect time and place. Beth, please. I need you."

"I know you do. But my first time will involve someone who cares for me, not just needs me."

"What do I have to do to prove myself to you?"

"I haven't decided," said Beth.

"Well, please decide soon. My God, but the effect you have on me. And I know you felt it too."

"What I think, feel, or want is not the point here. You need to prove that you have feelings for me."

"But I do. I swear I do. Tell me how to prove it?"

"Only you can figure that out."

"Beth, I don't play games."

"Neither do I."

"Fair enough. I'll say good night."

"Sleep well, Evie."

Evie lay in her bed in the guest room and relived the make out session. She was a hot, throbbing mess. She knew she could bring herself relief and it would feel good. But it would be empty relief. No, she'd wait. Beth was the only one who could really scratch her itch. Damn. Why was she so stubborn?

But Beth had been stubborn from the first moment they'd met. She'd been annoying and hardheaded. It seemed nothing had changed.

Evie finally fell asleep where she had erotic dreams all night long. Mysterious women had pleasured her. Many of them, mostly faceless women. Until Beth had shown up and banished all the others. Beth had pleased her like she'd never been pleased before.

Evie woke up drenched in sweat. She got up, took a shower, then dressed in jeans and a hoodie. She wanted to wear a blouse with a plunging neckline to tease Beth, but it was too cold.

She found Beth sitting at the table eating breakfast. She walked over and kissed the top of her hair. It was still damp from Beth's shower and Evie longed for the day they'd take their showers together. What a way to start a day.

"What was that for?" Beth said.

"I felt like it."

"Fair enough." But the look Beth gave Evie gave nothing away. No thoughts, no feelings. Nothing.

Evie knew she'd have an uphill battle to win Beth's heart. She just wished she knew where to start.

CHAPTER TWENTY-FOUR

I need to go to the library," Beth said. It was Monday and she couldn't imagine being in the house with Evie for the whole day. Not because she didn't like her. But because she did. Oh, so much. She'd replayed their major make out session over and over and it got her feeling things she'd never felt before. She really liked Evie, but she also wanted her and needed her. She wasn't used to these feelings and decided to distance herself from Evie as much as possible.

"I'll go with," said Evie.

"Why?"

"I haven't been inside a library since I graduated. I'd love to lose myself in a stack of books. You won't even know I'm there. Let me get my coat."

Shit. She didn't want to be in a car with Evie. That would mean being too close. Way too close. But how could she say no without looking like a complete asshole?

Evie was back with her coat on.

"I'm driving," said Beth.

"Fair enough. You want to drive my car?"

Beth thought about it. Evie's car was a much smoother ride than her truck. What would it hurt?

"Sure," she said.

As she maneuvered the Mercedes through town, she was surprised when Evie rested her hand on her leg.

"What are you doing?" said Beth.

"Establishing physical contact. I like touching you, Beth. I wish I could hold your hand or be touching you all the time."

"You really want to just fuck me, right? Is that it?"

"That's not even close. Not anywhere near close to what I want."

Beth parked the car in the library lot.

"We're here."

"Great. I'm going to explore while you work. Just text me when you're ready to leave."

"You got it."

The library was fairly empty on the first day of Thanksgiving break. Beth found a four-person table and sat down to spread out her books and get some studying done. She was working on algebra a couple of hours later when Evie sat next to her.

"I'm not ready to leave yet," Beth said.

"Nor am I. I found some books to read while you work."

Beth looked to see what books Evie had. *How To Win Friends and Influence People*, *Surrounded by Idiots*, and *Exactly What To Say*.

"Do those help you manipulate people to the best of your ability?" said Beth.

Evie's smile faltered, but she recovered quickly.

"Silly, they're important for building business relationships. Why are you working on algebra? I thought you were a business major?"

"I am. But I'm just taking general ed right now. We'll get into business classes next semester."

"Ah. Got it. What are you going to do with your degree?"

"I don't know. I'll find something."

"You could come work at my company," said Evie.

"In Dallas?"

"Yes, in Dallas. It's not an evil empire, you know?"

"If you say so."

"I do. You could be a paid intern at first to see how you like it. Oh, Beth. Say you will."

"I'll think about it," said Beth.

"I'll take that for now. Now, you study and let me read."

Beth tried to get back into algebra, but found her focus was lost. Evie's nearness, the smell of her perfume, everything about her distracted Beth. She was well aware of the desire she was feeling to kiss Evie all over and hear Evie's breathing become labored the more aroused she became.

She realized her line of thinking wasn't helping anything so put away her algebra and started working on a creative writing assignment. She stared at the blank page on her laptop, uncertain where to start.

"What's the theme of this assignment?" said Evie.

"A holiday romance."

"Write about us."

"I wouldn't exactly call us a romance."

"Then what would you call us?"

"A hot mess."

Evie went back to her reading and Beth considered what Evie had said. Why not make them into a holiday romance? Beth could assume the role of the man and Evie the woman. And she could give them a happily ever after. One that wasn't about to happen in real life.

She briefly contemplated writing a lesbian romance, but wasn't ready. She barely admitted to herself that she was gay. She didn't even know she was. She just might be attracted to Evie as a one-off.

So she settled in to write and was lost in the story when she heard Evie's stomach growl. Loudly. She laughed and looked over at Evie.

"Hungry much?"

"I'm sorry. I am getting hungry though."

"You think? Let's get home. We have plenty of food there to calm your angry beast."

Evie laughed and Beth's heart leaped to her throat. The sound of Evie's laughter did almost as much for her as Evie's kisses. Damn. Evie was dangerous.

They got home and Kelsey was nowhere to be found. Beth shot her a text. Kelsey responded almost immediately.

Lunch date. He's amazing. Home later.

"What?" Evie said when Beth read the text to her. "Who the hell is she having lunch with? And since when did she have dates?"

"Good questions. I suppose we'll find out when she gets home. Now let's eat."

Evie made them each a sandwich and served chips with them.

"You want a beer?" she said.

"Yes, please."

Evie got Beth a beer and poured herself a glass of wine. They ate in silence and after, Evie suggested a Trivial Pursuit rematch.

"What? Without Kelsey?"

"Yep. Just you and me, Beth. What do you say?"

"Bring it." Beth grinned. "You're clearly a glutton for punishment."

"Clearly." Evie laughed.

The game was still going strong when Kelsey got home.

"Time out," said Evie. "Let's hear about this mystery man."

"Yeah," said Beth. "And why didn't you tell us you had a date?"

"Because I didn't have one this morning. I met Chris at the grocery store. He's new to town and was trying to find things. I showed him around and helped him out and he asked me out to lunch."

"Was it a thank you lunch? Or a date-date lunch?"

"Oh, it was a date." Kelsey beamed. "And I invited him over for Thanksgiving. Hope that's okay?"

"That's great," said Evie as she hugged her tight. "That's wonderful."

"And maybe you two can pull your heads out so we can be two couples celebrating together."

"Watch it," said Beth. "I wouldn't get my hopes up."

"But I will," said Evie.

"As will I," Kelsey said.

"I need to finish my homework." Beth got up and headed to her room.

"But what about the game?"

"Kelsey can take my place."

As soon as Beth's door was closed, Kelsey sat down across from Evie.

"What the hell is her problem? Why is she so fucking stubborn?"

"I wish I knew, Kelsey. All I want for the holidays is her. But I don't know how to get it through her thick skull."

"I'd love to help, but she won't listen to me."

"She won't listen to anybody. She thinks I tricked her into falling for me. But I didn't. I swear. The last thing I had in mind when I came to this godforsaken part of Texas was finding a hot butch with no clue she was a lesbian who also happened to be a virgin and discovering she was the woman of my dreams."

Kelsey laughed.

"Right?! So are we going to play this game or what?"

"Or what for now. I'm going in to talk some sense into Beth. Wish me luck."

"Oh man. I wish you all the luck. You're going to need it."

Evie took a deep breath and knocked on Beth's door.

"Hm?"

"It's me. Can I come in?"

"Sure."

She opened the door to find Beth lying on her back in bed, hands clasped behind her head.

"I thought you were doing homework."

"I'm plotting," said Beth.

"Scoot over."

Beth moved to her left and Evie lay on her side, facing Beth. She rested her arm across Beth's chest.

"Mm. This is nice, isn't it?" said Evie.

"Evie…"

"Sh. Just relax."

Evie kissed Beth's jaw and nibbled on her ear. Then she kissed her cheek before finding Beth's parted lips. When Beth arched up and claimed Evie's mouth, Evie's heart soared. She was crazy about Beth Richards and needed some way to finally convince her of that. Until then, she'd take these mini make out sessions.

Beth rolled over and attempted to lie on top of Evie, but Evie gently eased her off. Evie climbed atop Beth and straddled her waist. She bent low to continue their kissing while Beth stroked her arms and back and Evie thought she would climax simply from those light touches.

Frustrated and aroused beyond anything she'd ever experienced, Evie took one of Beth's hands and placed it over her aching breast. Beth froze for a second before gently squeezing and kneading her, until Evie's nipples could have cut glass.

Evie moaned and straightened. She took her sweater over her head and threw it on the floor. Beth's eyes widened with appreciation and Evie fought the desire to get rid of her bra as well. Baby steps, damn it. Baby steps.

Beth sat up as best she could and took one of Evie's breasts in her mouth, bra and all. Evie leaned forward on her arms to let Beth have total access.

"Damn you feel good," Evie said. "You feel so good. Take my bra off, Beth. Dear God, please."

Beth fumbled for a few minutes, but finally Evie's breasts were free.

"Oh, shit," Beth said. "Oh, holy shit. They're beautiful. They're perfect."

She sucked one then the other nipple and Evie was teetering close to the brink.

"Will you make love to me, Beth? I mean, really make love to me?"

Beth lay flat.

"I can't. I'm sorry."

"What are you afraid of? I won't hurt you. You won't hurt me. We both need this."

"Maybe not physically, but emotionally you can do a lot of damage to me."

"Please. I know you have a hard time trusting me, but I'm begging you to let that go. Give yourself to me just like I want to give myself to you. Totally and completely."

"I can't do that. I've told you that."

"What do you want from me? How can I show you that I mean it?"

"I wish I knew. Now you'd better put yourself together and go chat with Kelsey or take a cold shower or whatever you need to do. I need some time to think. I need to clear my head and you sitting there half-naked isn't helping me."

"We could just make out some more."

"No. You need to get dressed."

Evie was crushed. She was fighting tears as she put her bra and sweater back on. She looked down at Beth, knowing her eyes were wet.

"I wish I could let you see how much you mean to me."

"So do I. I wish I could see inside your heart to know if I'm just a toy for you. But I can't, so you'll just have to give me time to see if I can learn to trust you."

Evie bent and kissed Beth. A tear slipped out and dropped onto Beth's cheek. Beth reached up and wiped it tenderly.

"Are you crying?" Beth said.

"I'm trying not to."

"But why?"

"Every time you push me away, it hurts like hell. I've fallen hard for you and it pains me that you don't or won't or can't return my feelings. I can't help it. I'll see you in a little while, Beth."

She left Beth's room and barely made it to her own before the tears started streaming uncontrollably. She threw herself on the bed and sobbed and sobbed. She felt sorry for herself that Beth didn't care about her, but then reasoned she probably really did. But she was frustrated that she couldn't convince Beth to relax and open up to what Evie was sure would be an awesome thing.

CHAPTER TWENTY-FIVE

Beth woke Thursday morning and inhaled the wonderful smell of delicious food cooking. She didn't know what exactly she smelled, but it made her stomach growl. She pulled on a robe and padded to the kitchen to find the counters laden with casseroles and pies.

"Damn. Y'all have been busy," she said.

"About time you got your lazy bones out of bed." Evie kissed her cheek. "We've been up for hours."

"So I see." But Beth couldn't think straight. The simple act of Evie kissing her cheek had her senses reeling. And she'd done it right in front of Kelsey who hadn't batted an eyelash.

"Happy Thanksgiving, Beth," said Kelsey.

"Happy Thanksgiving. All this food looks and smells amazing. But am I allowed to have breakfast? Because I'm famished."

"Sure, babe," said Evie. "Sit down. I'll make us all some bacon and eggs."

Beth poured a cup of coffee and sat at the dining room table where she could watch Evie. Kelsey came and sat at her usual spot.

"She's crazy about you, you know?" said Kelsey.

"I don't know."

"She has to leave soon to go back to Dallas for good, so don't drag your feet too long."

Beth felt like she'd been punched in the gut. Evie leaving? Sure, logically, she knew it would happen, but emotionally she wasn't ready to face that fact.

"You don't understand." Kelsey would never understand.

"You're right. I don't. You two are the world's cutest couple. And before, when y'all were sneaking around behind everyone's back trying to be sly, you were the happiest I've ever seen you."

"She manipulated me. It was all a game to her."

"I disagree. I think that's an easy excuse for you to hold on to because you're scared of your feelings," said Kelsey. "But I don't believe that for one minute."

"She had a file on me, Kels. A thick file with everything about me in it. She used that to get me to fall for her."

"Maybe she did have a file. I'm sure she did a ton of research on you before she approached you to sell the farm. But, she didn't use that information to trick you in any way. Her feelings for you are real, Beth. You need to stop being so stubborn."

Beth leaned against the back of her chair. Was she being overly stubborn? How badly could she get hurt if she gave herself freely to Evie? She'd think about it. But she wasn't ready to make any promises to anybody.

Evie joined them at the table.

"What time does Mr. Wonderful get here?" she said.

"Around two. I need you two on your best behavior. I can't have you scaring him off." She laughed.

"Should we make ourselves scarce so you two can be alone?" Evie winked at Beth whose stomach tightened.

"Oh, aren't you funny? I've told him all about you two star-crossed lovers. He'll be expecting to meet you both."

"Sounds good," said Evie.

"Yeah. I can't wait to meet him," Beth said.

"I better serve breakfast before I burn the bacon." Evie went back to the kitchen.

"She's crazy about you," Kelsey repeated.

"Yeah, yeah, yeah."

After breakfast, Beth took a long, hot shower and tried to calm her rushing hormones and thumping heart. What was she so afraid of? Yes, it hurt when she'd found that file on herself at Evie's that night. But what Kelsey said made sense. It was just what Evie had said, as a matter of fact.

If things didn't work out, though, could she stand the pain of losing Evie again? Was it worth finding out? And there and then she decided it was. She would indeed take that leap and see if they could make a go of it.

The relief she felt was overwhelming. She smiled as she rinsed off and she took her time dressing to make sure she looked good for Evie. Evie was all that mattered, all that had mattered for months.

"You look very handsome," said Evie when Beth walked out to the kitchen. "Like, yowza, Be still my foolish heart."

"Thanks." Beth kissed Evie's cheek.

"You two want to disappear for a few hours? I've got the kitchen under control," Kelsey said.

"No," said Beth.

"Sure," said Evie.

They both laughed.

"Now's not the time," Beth said. "Chris should be here any minute now."

"We still have some time. But if it's okay with y'all, I'm going to hop in the shower."

"Go for it."

Alone in the kitchen with Evie, Beth didn't know what to do or where to start. Evie was standing there looking at her and Beth figured, what the hell? She placed her hands on Evie's cheeks and gently pulled her close. When their lips met, it was like fireworks for Beth. It was like their first kiss all over again.

"What was that for?" said Evie. "Have you finally come to your senses?"

"I believe I may have."

"Oh, Beth. God, I hope you mean that."

Beth laughed nervously.

"Me, too."

"Look at you looking all debonair and whatnot and me a sweaty mess from cooking all morning."

"You look great."

"Thank you. But I know better. Now help me get this kitchen cleaned up before Chris gets here."

They worked together and got the kitchen spick-and-span. Kelsey came out clean from her shower and Evie decided to jump in herself.

"Would you like to join me?" she asked Beth.

"I've already had my shower today. Thanks, though."

Chris arrived while Evie was in the shower. He was a tall, thin cowboy who took his hat off when he entered the house. That impressed Beth.

"Chris, this is my sister, Beth," said Kelsey.

"I've heard a lot about you," said Chris.

"And I you."

"And where's your not really, but maybe, love interest?"

"That would be Evie." Beth laughed. "She's in the shower."

"Ah," he drawled.

"Let's have a drink," Kelsey said. "Beer or wine, Chris?"

"Beer please."

"Coming right up."

"You two get comfy. I'll grab the drinks," said Beth.

Evie finished in the shower and carefully chose her clothes. She wanted to look good for Beth, really good. She wanted to be irresistibly attractive. She chose a long, black denim skirt and a tight, red sweater. She checked herself out in the full-length mirror. Not bad. She slipped on some black flats and decided she should definitely be able to seduce Beth. Tonight would be the night. She was sure.

She came out to the living room to find Kelsey and a man she presumed to be Chris cozied up on the loveseat and Beth sitting in the recliner.

"You must be Chris," she said.

He stood and extended his hand.

"And you must be Evie."

"Guilty as charged." She shook his hand. "It's a pleasure to meet you."

"Likewise."

"Looks like I'm behind you all. I'd better get some vino. I'll be right back. Anybody need a refill?"

When she came back in the room with her wine, she fought the urge to sit on Beth's lap. She wanted to be close to her, to be touching her. But that wasn't going to happen with her in the recliner.

"Beth?" she said. "Why don't you join me on the couch?"

"Sure thing."

Evie expected Beth to sit at one end and her on the other, but Beth sat right up against her and draped her arm over Evie's shoulders.

"This is nice," Evie said.

"I don't mean to jinx anything going on here," said Chris. "But, aren't y'all supposed to be acting like you hate each other?"

"Not anymore." Evie thought her face would split from how wide she was smiling. "We're past that. Finally."

"Yeah we are," Beth said.

"That's great. So we're just a couple of couples celebrating Thanksgiving then, huh?"

"So it would seem."

Evie tried to relax and enjoy the conversation, but she was hyperaware of Beth's nearness, of her touch, of everything about her. They all chatted amicably with Beth asking Chris about himself and Chris asking questions about Evie and Beth. She was surprised and slightly bummed when she heard the oven buzz.

"Time to check the turkey," said Evie. "If you'll excuse me."

"I'll help." Beth jumped up off the couch.

"Great."

Alone in the kitchen, Evie slid her arms around Beth's neck.

"Don't you have to check the turkey?" Beth said.

"I can't concentrate on that or anything. I need you to kiss me."

Beth kissed her then. A powerfully passionate kiss that made Evie's toes curl. They held each other tight and Evie was completely lost in the moment. Until Kelsey cleared her throat.

"Will you be coming up for air any time soon?" she said.

Evie stepped back.

"Sorry."

"No. It's good. It makes me happy. But don't forget the bird."

"Oh, shit. That's right."

Beth turned off the obnoxious buzzer and Evie declared the turkey was ready. She spanked Beth lightly.

"No more distractions for me. I have work to do while the turkey cools. You get back out to the living room, please."

"Yes, ma'am," said Beth. "Anything you say."

Dinner went off without a hitch. Everyone said everything was delicious, but what made Evie the happiest was watching Beth devouring everything on her plate and refilling it. Evie had no intention of spending the rest of her life in a kitchen, but it was nice to know Beth appreciated her cooking.

"Did anyone save room for dessert?" Kelsey said.

"Oh, my God. I so forgot about dessert," said Beth.

"Maybe we can revisit that idea in a bit?" Chris said.

"Okay," said Kelsey. "We have three pies so make some room."

"Oh, my God," said Chris. "Three pies? I'm never eating again after I leave here."

They went back to the living room.

"Actually," said Chris, "I'd like to go for a walk. You up for that?"

"Sure," said Kelsey. "I'll get a coat."

After they left, Beth pulled Evie into a hug.

"Why don't you relax on the couch while I clear the table?"

"Don't be silly. I'll help."

"I insist."

Evie lay on the couch, completely relaxed and stuffed to the gills. She actually dozed for a few before she woke to Beth lying on top of her.

"What are you doing?" Evie said.

"Getting comfortable."

"Mm. I do like the sound of that."

Beth kissed her then. It was a tender kiss, but Evie wanted, needed more. She ran her tongue along Beth's lips until they parted so her tongue could meander into Beth's mouth. Beth's tongue met hers and they frolicked together for what seemed an eternity. But Evie wasn't complaining. She couldn't get enough.

Through the fog of desire, Evie became aware that Beth was grinding her pelvis into her. Evie wrapped her legs around Beth's ass and pressed her into her. And then she heard the front door close.

"Sit up," Evie said. "Come on, look decent."

"Shit." Beth sat and Evie snuggled against her.

"How was your walk?" Evie said.

"Cold. Bitterly cold. But nice. Shall we have pie?"

"Sounds good," Beth said.

Evie stood on shaky legs and followed Kelsey into the kitchen.

"You look guilty as hell." Kelsey laughed.

"We were only kissing."

"Yeah. Sure."

They served the pie and after dessert, Chris stretched.

"This has been a fantastic day," he said. "But I have to work tomorrow, so I'd better get going."

"You sure you won't stay?" said Evie. "I'm sure Kelsey wouldn't mind."

Chris beamed.

"Tempting though that may be, it's not a good idea. Not tonight."

"Why not come over tomorrow night for leftovers?" said Beth.

"That's up to Kelsey," he said.

"I'd love it," Kelsey said. "Now let me walk you out to your truck."

"Don't be silly. You'll catch your death of pneumonia. Tell me good-bye at the front door, please."

"Let's give them some privacy." Evie took Beth's hand and led her back to the couch. "Now, where were we?"

CHAPTER TWENTY-SIX

Beth forgot where she was as she and Evie picked up where they'd left off. Her brain was on fire as was the rest of her body. She was feeling things she'd never even dared to fantasize about.

She knew she needed more but wasn't entirely sure what that meant. She only knew she couldn't just stay on the couch kissing Evie. As if reading her mind, Evie spoke.

"Let's go to your room."

"Hm?" She'd heard Evie but was unable to process what she'd said.

"Take me to bed, Beth. Please. Before you change your mind."

"I'm not changing my mind. Come on. Let's go."

"You two need to get a room," Kelsey said.

"Kels," said Beth, feeling like a bucket of ice had been poured over her.

"Yes?" said Kelsey. "I'm still here, but I'm going to bed. I think y'all should do the same."

"Good night, Kelsey," said Evie.

"Good night you two. Have fun." She winked at Beth who felt her cheeks heat. She wasn't one for blushing, but she felt like she'd been busted and didn't like the feeling.

She stood and Evie took her hand and pulled her back to the couch.

"Are you okay?" Evie said.

"Yeah. Fine."

"No, you're not. You're upset that we got caught. But listen to me, Beth. Kelsey is all for us getting together. She wants you to be happy and believes I can help with that. I don't want you to close off now. Please, God. Don't close off now."

"I'm sorry," Beth said. "She…well…I don't know. It's just that was so awkward."

"It doesn't need to be. We're two grown adults doing what grown adults do. She gets that. Did she ever just shut down after spending the night at some random guy's house?"

"No."

"Did you judge her?"

"No," said Beth.

"See? It's the same thing. Now, are you going to be okay?"

"I need a drink."

"I don't want you getting buzzed, Beth. I have plans for you and I want you to be a full participant."

"I'll just grab a beer. I'll get you a glass of wine."

She took a deep breath when she was alone in the kitchen. Was she ready? Was she actually ready to take the next step with Evie? She didn't feel like she was. Then she thought back to how she felt when laying on top of Evie on the couch. When kissing Evie. And she knew she was ready. Kelsey be damned.

Evie looked at Beth questioningly when she showed up in the living room without drinks.

"Did you forget something?" Evie laughed.

"No. Come on. Let's go to bed."

"Now you're talking."

Evie took Beth's hand and they walked to Beth's bedroom.

"It's kind of a mess," said Beth.

"You are so fucking cute. I've seen your bedroom, babe. Remember?"

"Well, why don't you sit on my bed and let me pick up a bit."

Beth had clothes strewn all over. She didn't want to admit to Evie how many times she'd changed her clothes that morning in an attempt to look her best for her. She quickly picked up the clothes and threw them in the closet. She'd deal with them later.

She sat on the bed and Evie took her hand in both of hers.

"You okay?" she said. Beth nodded. "I mean it. I don't want to force you into anything."

"You're not. I'm coming willingly."

"You will be soon." Evie laughed.

"I just…it's just…I know I need more. I have to have more with you. More than just kissing on the couch. But I'm not sure what more is. I don't know what I want or what to do."

There. She'd said it.

"Babe, you just do what makes you feel good."

"But I want you to feel good, too," said Beth.

"Oh, I will. You're going to make me see stars. I know it. One nice thing about being with a woman is you know how to please me already. Any time you've masturbated, you've practiced pleasing me."

Beth was silent. Absolutely still.

"Beth? Have you ever masturbated?"

Beth shook her head.

"Okay. That's fine. You just explore my body then, okay? You touch where you want to and check things out. I'll help, but I really want you to be the source of my pleasure. Does that sound fair?"

"How did I get so lucky to find you?"

"I think I'm the lucky one, babe."

Beth kissed Evie again, fiercely and possessively. Evie kissed her back with equal fervor. Beth felt herself trembling as parts of her sprung to life that had been dormant for thirty-two years.

Evie lay back and Beth climbed on top of her. She propped herself on her elbows and stared into Evie's dark eyes.

"You're beautiful, you know that?" said Beth.

"You're going to make me blush."

They kissed for a long while before Beth flashed back to the night she'd had Evie topless. She needed that again. As they continued kissing, Beth tugged on the bottom of Evie's sweater and finally got it over her head.

She kissed down Evie's neck and licked her chest. She needed to feel Evie's nipples in her mouth again, but didn't want to rush. She wanted to take her time and make this night last forever. After all, it wasn't every night one lost their virginity to the most beautiful woman on the planet.

Beth nipped at Evie's bra, biting her nipples with her lips and watching in amazement as they grew and grew.

"Let me get this off," muttered Evie. Beth climbed off just long enough for Evie to remove her bra before lying down again. She stared at the long, puckered nubs and knew she needed to taste them.

She ran her tongue over one erect nipple then the other. She loved the feel of the hardness against her tongue. She finally closed her mouth over one and sucked hard. She wanted to suck with all her might but didn't know how hard would be too much.

"Oh dear God." Evie arched into her mouth. "Oh, damn that feels good. I need to feel you, Beth. Don't stop what you're doing. I'm going to get you out of your shirt."

Beth thought briefly she should help, but she wasn't about to stop suckling Evie. Evie's breasts were small but pert and Beth wanted to stay where she was all night. She was only vaguely aware of Evie unbuttoning her shirt.

"Oh, God," Evie moaned. "Oh fuck. Beth? Babe? Hold on one sec. Let's get you out of that shirt."

She pushed the shirt off Beth and helped her get it off completely.

"Now, you lose your bra," Evie said.

Beth took off her sports bra and looked at Evie who was eying Beth's chest like she was at a smorgasbord.

She lay back down and the feel of skin on skin almost made her head explode. Evie's hard nipples were poking into her own tiny nipples which had never been this hard before. She rubbed them back and forth on Evie's breasts and Evie moaned again.

"Damn, Beth. You're going to get me off with nipple play."

"Is that a bad thing?"

"Oh, no, sweetheart. That's a very good thing."

Beth kissed back to Evie's mouth and as they kissed, she became aware that Evie was bucking against her. Softly and slowly, but she was obviously ready for more. Was Beth?

And then Beth knew she had to see Evie naked. Completely clothes-less for her inspection. She'd never seen a grown woman naked save for herself and she had a feeling she was in for a real treat.

She reached behind Evie and unzipped her skirt. Evie kicked off her shoes and helped Beth pull her skirt off. Evie lay there in just her thong and Beth felt the blood rushing in her ears. Evie was perfect and she was Beth's. All Beth's.

Beth peeled off the thong and sat staring at Evie.

"My God, you're gorgeous."

"Why don't you get undressed too, Beth? I want to lie naked with you. I want to feel every inch of your body against mine."

Beth stood and almost fell over. She was dizzy and shaky, but knew if Evie wanted her naked, she was going to get naked for her. She got her jeans off.

She stepped out of her underwear and lay next to Evie.

"Lay on top of me again. Please?" said Evie.

"Okay." Beth took one last look at Evie's perfect physique before laying on top of her again."

"Oh, shit," said Evie. "You feel amazing."

"Mm. As do you. Your skin is so silky soft. I need to touch you, though. I'm going to roll off you again, okay?"

"Sure."

Beth lay against Evie and dragged her hand over Evie's breasts, belly, and thighs. Evie spread her legs, but Beth was still unsure of what she was supposed to do. She dragged her hand along Evie's soft inner thighs and soon Evie was mewling.

"I need you to touch me, Beth."

"I am touching you."

"Between my legs, please."

Beth looked at Evie then. She looked between her legs and saw a pink shimmering heaven waiting for her. She placed her hand between Evie's legs and felt how wet she was. The evidence of Beth's arousal was dripping down her own thighs.

She played with Evie's inner lips, gently tugging on them. But it was when she found Evie's tight center that she almost lost it. Instinctively, Beth plunged a finger deep and stroked Evie's satin walls on the way out.

"I need more, babe. More fingers. Don't be afraid."

Beth slipped another finger inside. And then another.

"Perfect," breathed Evie.

Beth drove her fingers as deep as she could and twisted and turned them as she pulled them out. She repeated her actions and soon Evie was holding her wrist while she bucked against Beth.

"Don't stop, baby. Oh, God I'm close."

Beth, emboldened by Evie's response, bent and sucked a nipple while she continued driving as deep as she could get inside her.

"So close," whispered Evie. "Oh God, Beth. You make me feel so good."

Beth was barely aware of Evie's speaking. She was in such a hyper aroused state herself.

"Oh fuck," Evie screamed. "Oh fuck I'm coming."

Beth felt Evie's center tighten around her. She closed down on Beth's fingers in a death grip. Beth had never experienced such a wonderful sensation.

Evie lay breathing heavily.

"So are we through then?" said Beth.

"Not even close. We're just warming up. Now, lie back and let me please you."

Beth couldn't imagine anything better. She had never had an orgasm before but if it felt as good as Evie seemed to feel, she was all over it. She rolled over onto her back and Evie climbed atop her. Feeling Evie's wetness on her belly had Beth throbbing even harder.

Evie kissed Beth while her fingers found Beth's nipples. Damn. Beth's nipples seemed to be hardwired to between her legs because every tweak got her wetter.

Beth lay taut with anticipation, waiting for Evie to suck her or touch her between her legs. Something, anything to ease this madness. It was pleasure but she felt like she was losing her mind from all the sensations she was experiencing at once.

Evie suckled Beth then and Beth cried out from how good it felt. Evie knew what she was doing with her tongue. She kept circling Beth's nipples even as she drew them hard into her mouth.

Beth lost all track of time. Evie could have been sucking her nipples for five minutes. Or an hour. Or five hours. But eventually Evie released her grip on Beth's nipples and kissed down her stomach. She moved lower until she was straddling one of Beth's legs.

Beth opened her eyes and looked at Evie who was looking longingly between Beth's legs.

Chapter Twenty-seven

Beth didn't have time to appreciate how incredibly sexy Evie looked before Evie dipped her head and licked between Beth's legs. The feel of her tongue there felt at once dirty and amazing. She'd never bothered to wonder about oral sex. She'd never really thought about sex before. But now she wanted to return the favor. She needed to taste Evie in a big way.

Thoughts flew from her head as Evie let her talented tongue loose inside Beth. Beth squirmed and writhed, needing more but not sure what that was. Then Evie did something that rocked Beth's world. She dragged her tongue over Beth's clit. It felt amazing.

"Oh shit," Beth said. "Oh holy shit."

But the best was yet to come. Evie's lips closed around her clit while her tongue continued to stroke her. And then, just like that, Evie slid her fingers inside Beth. Beth felt filled and teetering on the edge of a precipice she only hoped Evie would topple her into.

Suddenly Beth was aware of nothing but Evie's tongue and fingers. All coherent thought abandoned her. She didn't realize she was moving her hips in time to Evie's fingers moving in and out of her.

All her energy focused on her center and the feelings Evie was creating. Beth felt herself edging close to losing it yet she wasn't afraid. She went with it. Her whole body tensed then white heat shot through her limbs. The world disappeared into myriad colors. She felt better than she ever had when she finally settled back into her body.

She didn't know how much time had passed. She only became aware that Evie was curled up next to her. She wrapped her arm around her and hugged her tight.

"Damn," Beth said. "Damn, damn, damn."

"You okay?"

"Hell yeah. So that's what I've been missing all these years."

Evie chuckled.

"Indeed it is."

"Wow."

"I'd like to think it felt better because it was me," said Evie.

"I'm sure that had a lot to do with it."

"Good."

Beth dozed for a few and awoke to Evie stroking her chest.

"I'm sorry I fell asleep."

"That's okay. I slept too."

Beth rolled on top of Evie and kissed her hard on her mouth. She was worked up again and needed to please Evie another time. She had to make her feel those things that she'd made Beth feel.

She kissed and nibbled down Evie's neck and chest and finally stopped to gaze longingly at her perfect breasts. She took a nipple in her mouth and Evie gasped.

"You okay?" said Beth.

"Oh God yes."

Beth moved up so she could look Evie in the eye.

"May I try that?"

"What?" said Evie.

"What you did to me."

"I don't understand."

"May I use my mouth on you?" Beth said.

"God, I wish you would."

Beth climbed between Evie's legs. She stared at the wet feast before her and wondered where to begin. She dragged her tongue from Evie's clit to the opening of her soul. She buried her tongue deep inside and lapped at all the juices flowing there.

Evie tasted amazing. The flavor was hard to describe. It was unlike anything Beth had ever tasted but she couldn't get enough. Evie was musky and salty and sweet all at once.

By the time Beth licked back to Evie's clit, it was swollen to twice the size it had started. This made Beth smile. She circled it with her tongue before closing her lips over it and flicking its tender underside with her tongue.

Evie played her fingers through Beth's hair as Beth settled in. She'd found heaven and was never leaving. She was only vaguely aware of Evie's touch so lost was she in pleasuring her.

Evie's grip tightened as she arched into Beth's mouth. Up and down her hips moved and Beth struggled to hold on. She finally sucked hard on Evie's clit and ran her tongue all over it and Evie screamed as she found her release.

"Damn," Evie said when she found her breath. "You're a natural."

"I want to do that all day every day."

"You won't get any complaints from me."

Evie cuddled against Beth again, but couldn't stay still long. She had to take Beth again. Had to give Beth more of the pleasure she'd been denying herself for thirty-two years. This time she pleased Beth with her fingers as she sucked her nipples. She plunged them in and out over and over before rubbing her clit. She was rewarded when Beth let out a guttural moan as she climaxed.

Evie woke in the morning to an empty bed. She panicked, wondering if she'd scared Beth off. She checked her phone on the nightstand and saw it was nine o'clock. How could she have slept so late?

She got up and dressed then went out to the kitchen where she found Beth and Kelsey sipping coffee.

"Nice outfit," Kelsey said.

Evie looked down at the same clothes she'd been wearing the day before and shrugged.

"I think she looks wonderful." Beth crossed the room and kissed Evie tenderly.

"Thank you. I worried when I woke all alone."

"Sorry. You were sound asleep and I didn't want to disturb you, so I snuck out."

"As long as I didn't scare you off," said Evie.

"Not a chance."

"I'm famished," Evie said. "I know we have a shit ton of leftovers, but let me buy us breakfast."

"Finally," said Kelsey. "Something I care about."

Beth and Evie laughed.

They got dressed and Evie treated them to breakfast at their favorite greasy spoon.

"So are you two finally together, together? Or will you be doing something stupid again?"

Evie held her breath as she looked at Beth and waited for her to answer.

"We're together, together," Beth said.

"Yay! This makes me so happy," Kelsey said. "So very happy."

"Me, too," Evie said softly. "Me, too."

Back in the house, Kelsey yawned.

"I think I'm going to take a nap before I head over to Chris's. I'll catch y'all later."

"Oh man, a nap sounds great," Evie said.

"You should take one then," said Beth.

"We could take one together."

Beth grinned.

"As much as I'd love that, I've got studying to do."

"Can I sleep in your bed?"

"Sure."

They held hands as they walked to Beth's room. Beth sat at her desk and opened her laptop. Evie took off her clothes.

"What are you doing?" Beth said.

"I can't sleep in clothes."

"How am I supposed to concentrate?"

Evie flashed her a wicked smile.

"Maybe you won't?"

"Oh, shit," said Beth. "I'm going to go out to the dining room."

"I admire how dedicated you are. I mean that."

"Thanks. It sure as hell isn't easy right now."

Evie was all horned up when Beth left the room. Yes, she was sleepy, but she also wanted Beth with an ache that was unfamiliar to her. She'd had more than her fair share of partners over the years, but none affected her like Beth. There was something about her…

She woke an hour later and stretched. The ache for Beth hadn't dissipated while she slept. She wanted, needed her now. She pulled on her skirt and sweater and went in search of her.

Beth was at the dining room table, textbooks strewn across it.

"Hey, gorgeous," said Evie.

"Hey there. How'd you sleep?"

"Mm. Like a baby. Someone wore me out last night."

Beth blushed. That was the first time Evie had seen her do that and she found her even more endearing.

"You're so stinkin' cute," said Evie. "So stinkin' cute."

"And you're drop-dead gorgeous, so I guess we're even?"

"I guess." Evie laughed. "Can you take a break from studying?"

"I think I'm at a good stopping point. What's up?"

"Come to bed with me?"

"Now?"

"Yeah. Is Kelsey still sleeping?"

"She actually left," said Beth. "She went over to Chris's. She won't be home until tomorrow."

"In that case." Evie took her sweater off. Beth's eyes widened as they took in Evie's bare breasts. Evie stepped out of her skirt and lowered herself onto Beth's lap, facing Beth. "Touch me, baby. I need you."

She leaned in and pressed her breasts against Beth, kissing her hard on her mouth. Beth met her passion in kissing her back, which only fanned the flame threatening to consume Evie.

"Touch me," Evie pleaded again.

Beth ran her hands up and down Evie's thighs. She dragged her thumbs along Evie's sensitive inner thighs and had her squirming on Beth's lap. She took Beth's hand and placed it between her legs.

"Damn, you're wet," Beth said.

"Very. I have an itch only you can scratch."

Beth buried her fingers deep inside and Evie arched to take her deeper.

"Dear God, you feel good," she gasped. "Please, keep going. Don't stop."

They kissed some more, and Evie's head was soon spinning at the myriad sensations. She leaned back and spread wider, urging Beth to fuck her faster and harder.

Beth leaned forward and sucked on Evie's nipple and Evie felt the earth tremble She tried to hold out a little longer, to enjoy the buildup. But she couldn't. Her world exploded into millions of tiny light fragments before it coalesced again and she floated back to her body.

"Let's get you out of these clothes," Evie whispered.

"Here? What if Kelsey and Chris come home?"

"That didn't seem to bother you a minute ago."

"Let's go to my room."

Satiated for the moment, Evie took her time with Beth. She kissed, sucked, and nibbled every inch of her. She committed each freckle, each mole to memory. She learned where Beth was ticklish and what really made her squirm.

"Please. You're making me crazy," said Beth.

"You've had enough teasing? Hm?"

"Yes! I need release. Please. Do something. I can't wait anymore."

"Show me what you like, Beth. Touch yourself for me."

"No," Beth said.

"Please? It would really turn me on."

"I-I-I wouldn't know how."

"Do you trust me?" asked Evie.

"Yes."

Evie took Beth's fingers and placed them on her clit. Evie kept her fingers on Beth's and together they rubbed the hard base of it.

"Oh, shit," said Beth. "Oh, holy shit."

"There." Evie was becoming more aroused by the moment. "Doesn't that feel good?"

"Oh, fuck yes."

"Keep it up. Don't stop. We'll get you there."

"Oh, I'm there." And Beth let out a guttural moan that seemed to come all the way from her toes. It was loud and long and music to Evie's ears.

"Dear God, that was hot." Evie watched Beth try to catch her breath. She brought Beth's fingers to her mouth and sucked them clean. "You taste divine."

"I do?"

"Oh yes. Simply divine."

"Can we nap now? That wore me out."

"I'm afraid I'm too keyed up to sleep. I have an idea though. You just stay right there on your back."

Evie lowered herself onto Beth's mouth. Beth immediately began to devour her. Evie soon moved all around on her face, grinding into her, lost in wanton abandonment as she lost control, left her body, and sailed into oblivion.

She climbed off Beth and snuggled against her, more content than she could ever recall being.

CHAPTER TWENTY-EIGHT

Beth woke a couple of hours later and gazed longingly at Evie's sleeping figure. She knew she should let her sleep, but really didn't want to. She was filled with an urge she was powerless to resist.

She climbed between Evie's legs and feasted on the hot pink flesh she found there. It wasn't long before Evie was awake and holding Beth's head in place. As if she was going anywhere.

Evie stiffened, cried out, and collapsed on the bed. Beth fought to not smile with pride. She enjoyed pleasing Evie. Very, very much. The fact that what she enjoyed so much brought such pleasure to Evie was just icing on the cake.

They showered together and enjoyed each other's bodies yet again. They dried each other off, got dressed, poured themselves drinks, and sat at the dining room table.

"I'm crazy about you, you know that, right?" Evie said.

"I hope so. I can't get enough of you."

"But I need to know you know how I feel."

"I think I do," said Beth.

"Great. Now, we need to have a talk and I figure sooner is better than waiting until the last minute."

Beth felt her heart drop to her stomach. Shit. She didn't know what was coming, but she suddenly felt like her mom took her favorite puppy to the pound.

"Okay. I'm listening."

"Beth, the reality is that I have to go back to Dallas. That's where my home is. That's where my life is. But I don't want to leave my heart here."

"I know you've got to go home. I just don't like to think about it. So where does that leave me?"

Evie took Beth's hands in hers.

"Come with me, Beth. I can get you a job in our company."

"I don't have a degree yet."

"You can work part-time and go to school. Finish your degree and move up."

"What about Kelsey?" said Beth.

"She's got Chris. Have you ever seen her happier? She'll be fine."

"And my house? And…"

"We can sort through all that," said Evie. "We don't have to finalize all the details right this second. But I don't want to leave without you. That's what we need to talk about."

"I wouldn't have a place to stay."

"Silly. You'll be staying with me."

Beth thought it over. That sounded wonderful. It all seemed like a great adventure that she deserved to go on. So what was holding her back?

"How smart would it be for me to work at your company?" said Beth.

"I have connections. If you don't want to work there, I can get you a job at another company. I'll take care of you, Beth. Please let me."

There it was. It all made sense to Beth in that statement.

"I'm used to being the one caring for everyone else. I don't know how I'd feel about being a kept woman."

"You won't be. We'll be partners. Equal partners. But I can help you get started. It'll be a big change for you. I get that. And I know you like being in charge. We both do. So that's something we'll have to work on. But I believe we can. I believe in us."

"You really do, don't you?"

"I do. Oh, Beth. I don't want to go back to Dallas without you. Please say you'll come with me."

"How about this? I can't come right now. But we can put things in place that'll get the ball rolling. And in a little while, I'll move."

"How soon is a little while?" Evie said.

"January?"

"That'll work. I'll take time off to spend the holidays with you all and then we'll move you to Dallas."

"That sounds good."

Evie circled the table and pulled Beth into a hug. The feel of Evie's body against her caused Beth to want her anew. She kissed Evie and Evie held her tighter. Beth couldn't tell where her body ended and Evie's began. And she never wanted the moment to end.

"This calls for champagne," said Evie. "Let's go get some."

Beth laughed. Evie, for being a strong, together business-woman, could sure act like a little kid at times.

"Okay, champagne it is," she said.

When they got home from the store, Beth got a fire going and they sat on the couch together.

"Isn't this nice?" said Evie.

"It really is."

"Our life can be like this all the time. From now on. When you're in Dallas, we'll be together every night."

"Really? Would you be content just hanging with me? Wouldn't you miss the nightlife?"

"I wouldn't need the nightlife, Beth. In you I've found everything I was ever looking for."

"You mean that?"

"I do."

Beth looked into the pools of chocolate that were Evie's eyes and saw so much there. Excitement, contentment, and something more. Something that made Evie shiver inside.

"What?" said Evie.

"I don't know. I just…I don't know what I want right now. I don't even know what I'm feeling."

"Do you feel good?"

"That doesn't begin to describe it," said Beth.

"Kiss me, Beth. Please kiss me."

Beth kissed her. Softly, gently, lovingly at first, but Evie obviously needed more. Soon Evie was on her back with Beth on top of her, grinding into her, needing more than to simply be kissing. She needed to touch Evie, to be touched by Evie.

Thoughts and desire coursed through her head. She was dizzy and aroused and her blood was rushing in her ears. She didn't hear the front door open and was mildly irritated to hear Kelsey calling her name.

She rolled off Evie and landed on the floor. Kelsey and Chris laughed, and it took a few seconds of deep breathing for Beth to be able to communicate clearly.

"What are you two doing here?"

"We have an announcement," said Kelsey.

"What's that?" Evie said.

"We're moving in together."

"What? This is happening rather quickly. Are you sure?"

"We're positive," said Chris. "I love this little lady and want her to live with me."

"We're going to start looking for a place. His apartment is too small for both of us."

"Live here," said Beth.

"No offense," Kelsey said. "But we'd like our own place."

"I'm moving to Dallas," Beth blurted.

"You're what? That's fantastic." Kelsey helped Beth off the floor and hugged her.

"Can I get in on this action?" Evie stood and started a group hug.

"I'm so happy for you two," said Kelsey. "So stinkin' happy. You two will be the best couple ever."

"Best lesbian couple," Chris said. "We're the best couple ever."

They all laughed.

Evie pulled away from the hug.

"We're having champagne. Join us?"

"We brought a bottle too." Chris held up the bottle they'd brought. "Let's get drunk."

"We're going to need food if we're going to drink two bottles of champagne," Evie said. "Come on."

She took Kelsey's hand and walked with her to the kitchen.

"Let's get everything heated up," Kelsey said. "Where should we start?"

"Turkey," Chris and Beth said together.

"What are you two doing here?" Kelsey said. "Evie and I got this. You two pour champagne."

"I'm so happy for you," Evie told Kelsey. "I'm glad that you finally found Mr. Right after all your searching."

"I don't know how hard I was searching. I was mostly just having fun. But this is different. This is real. But let's talk about you. How did you get my big sister to agree to move to Dallas?"

"It really wasn't that hard. I mean, yes, she resisted in the beginning. I think she's so used to being the responsible one, the caregiver if you will, that she can't fathom sharing that role with someone else. She can't wrap her head around the fact that I'll be there for her. To help her or whatever. She's having a hard time grasping that."

"Well, you'd better take great care of her or you'll have Chris and me to answer to."

"I'll take the very best care of her. She means the world to me," said Evie.

"I know this. And I believe you."

They served dinner and sat down with their respective partners.

"I'm so glad you two finally got over yourselves," Chris said. "From everything Kelsey had told me, I'd about given up hope."

Beth shot Kelsey a dirty look, but Evie just smiled.

"I don't care if you gave up hope. I never would," she said.

"So what are you going to do in Dallas?" Chris asked Beth.

"Finish my education," Beth said. "Then get a job. Start my career. And live happily ever after."

"Sounds wonderful," Kelsey said.

"So are y'all going to move in here?" said Evie.

"I don't know," said Chris. "I'd kind of like us to get our own place. Start out fresh. I don't want to seem ungrateful."

"That makes sense," said Beth. "We'll sell this place and split the money we get."

"You should keep the money," said Kelsey.

"No. It was the farm that paid for the house. That farm was the family's."

"You were the one who kept the farm going though. So you should keep the money."

"Let's revisit this after the sale happens," Evie interjected. "Let's not discuss it now."

After dinner, Kelsey and Evie did the dishes then Chris and Kelsey went back to Chris's place. Beth took Evie in her arms.

"What now, beautiful?"

"Bed," Evie said. "I need you so desperately."

"Mm. I'm here to help."

They undressed each other slowly, prolonging the inevitable. Evie stood naked in front of Beth feeling comfortable and confident that she was finally with the right woman. She'd been in a few relationships and had had who knows how many one-night stands? But this was different. This was real. This she felt in her bones.

She looked at Beth looking at her and melted inside. There was such tenderness, such caring, such…love? She didn't know but wanted to believe.

Beth closed the distance between them and kissed Evie hard on the mouth. They kissed for an eternity until Evie's head began to spin and she was about to fall over.

She lay on the bed and Beth lay beside her. Beth dragged her hand up and down Evie's body and Evie spread her legs as far as she could, silently pleading with Beth to touch her.

Beth was propped up on her elbow, looking into Evie's eyes as her fingers found her tight wet center. Evie stared back at Beth, wanting Beth to see in her eyes how much she was enjoying her and how crazy about her she truly was.

Try as she might, Evie couldn't keep her eyes open. The sensations Beth was creating were nudging her closer and closer to the edge of oblivion and all Evie could concentrate on was getting to the edge and soaring off it.

Beth may have been new to this lovemaking thing, but she knew just where to stroke Evie to drive her wild. Evie held her breath as she teetered, then screamed Beth's name as she found her release and was catapulted out of her body and into orbit. She floated back into her body and opened her eyes.

"You do amazing things to me," she said.

"You're fun to do things to." Beth grinned. "You're gorgeous, you know that? I want to watch you climax every time."

"Don't embarrass me. I'm sure I make a horrible face when I come."

"It's actually contorted for a second, then you have the most serene look after you scream. I love it."

"I love you."

"What?"

"I said I love you, Beth. You don't have to say it back. But I want you to know."

"Do you mean that?" said Beth.

"I do."

"I love you, too, Evie. I think I always have."

Evie kissed Beth and rolled on top of her, ready to show her again just how much she loved her.

Epilogue

It was a beautiful spring day in Vernon. The temperature was in the mid-seventies, the cloudless sky a lovely hue. It was the perfect day for a wedding. Two weddings made the day that much better.

"How you doin'?" Beth asked Chris in the groom's dressing room.

"Nervous as hell. You?"

"I'm pretty calm. I know I'm doing the right thing, you know?"

"But this is for forever."

"Is there anyone besides Kelsey you can imagine journeying into forever with?"

"Not a soul." He grinned.

"Then don't be nervous."

"I'll be right back."

Beth checked her reflection in the mirror. The Kelly green satin shirt she wore under her tux was Evie's favorite color. Her pocket square matched, and the cuff links and button covers were white gold. She'd found them in her dad's things and Evie had agreed she had to wear them.

She sat in a leather wingback chair and took a swig from her flask. She hadn't been completely honest with Chris. She was nervous. Terrified even. Not at the prospect of marriage. But the idea of standing in front of all those people is what made her knees knock.

"Oh, my God. There are a million people out there. It's standing room only." Chris looked paler than usual and Beth worried he might pass out.

"Here." She handed him her flask. He took a long pull.

"Thanks. I needed that."

"No problem. Now, do you remember your vows?"

"Shit. I hope so."

"Say them for me," Beth said. "Just to practice."

"No. I got 'em. I'd rather wait and say them to Kels."

"That makes sense."

There was a knock on the door.

"Are y'all decent?"

Beth recognized the voice of Rose, the wedding planner.

"We are," Chris said.

Rose opened the door.

"It's showtime."

Beth took another swig then put the flask in her pocket.

"Ready, Chris?" she said.

"What the hell? Let's do this."

Beth took her place at the altar and focused on not watching the crowd. There were hundreds of people there. Many of Evie's friends had made the trip from Dallas. And the whole population of Vernon and Walker seemed to be present. Chris wasn't kidding. The church was packed.

The organist played the opening strands of the "Wedding March" and Beth focused on the door at the far end of the church. Kelsey walked in first, escorted by Chris's dad.

When Evie appeared, Beth's heart caught in her throat. Never had she seen a more beautiful sight. Evie was wearing a long ivory gown with a plunging décolletage. Beth fell in love all over again in the moment. The guests were forgotten. She was here to pledge her love to this woman and she would do so proudly.

Robert was escorting Evie and when he handed her over to Beth, he said, "She's your problem now."

The three of them laughed and Beth gratefully took Evie and turned to the altar. She focused on everything they did, lighting the unity candle, joining their hands together. She even said her vows without a hitch. The wedding was perfect.

The couples danced to "Better Together" by Luke Combs. Halfway through the song, they opened the dance floor up to the guests. There was hardly room for everybody, but no one seemed to mind.

Evie led Beth out into the gardens after the song.

"What's up, baby girl?" Beth said.

"I just need some time with my wife. Is that okay?"

"That's great. But I didn't think you of all people would need a break from the crowds so soon."

"I love you, Beth. I know a big wedding isn't what you wanted and I want you to know how grateful I am to you."

"You're most welcome. My goal for the rest of our life together is to make you as happy as I can. I'll do whatever it takes. Besides, a big wedding means I get to see your boobs hanging out." She laughed.

"Does it look tacky?"

"Not at all. You look amazing."

Beth kissed Evie hard on her mouth. She plunged her tongue in her mouth and suddenly was overcome with need to have Evie every which way she could. Right then and there.

"Let's find someplace private," Beth managed breathlessly. "I need you."

"You can't get to me in this dress, babe. Sorry, but you'll have to wait until we get back to the hotel."

"Shit."

"I can take care of you, though."

"No, I'll tough it out. I mean I appreciate it, but I can wait."

They ate and danced and drank and danced some more. Rose approached them while they were resting between songs.

"It's time for y'all to think about leaving. Your guests will be getting ready to leave and they won't want to until you have."

"I'll go grab Chris and Kelsey," said Beth. "Then are you ready?"

Evie winked.

"I'm beyond ready."

Beth swallowed hard, turned, and on shaky legs went in search of her sister and her husband. Kelsey had a husband. That was something she'd never thought possible. But then she'd never imagined that she herself would have a wife. What a strange couple of years it had been.

She found them on the patio.

"Hey, lovebirds, let's do one more lap through the guests and then we've got to get going."

"You got it," said Chris.

"Time for the fairy tale to end?" said Kelsey.

"Babe, your fairy tale is only beginning."

"Good call, Chris," said Beth. "Now, come on. Let's hit it."

The limo ride to their hotel took little time and the four of them got in the elevator.

"Was it everything you had imagined?" Beth said.

"More," said Chris.

"It was magical," said Kelsey.

"I'll show you how special I thought it was," Evie said.

"Is that right?" Beth kissed her as the elevator came to a stop at the bridal suite.

Evie took Beth's hand and led her to the bed.

"Get me out of this dress. I need you to take me."

"I'll be sorry to see that dress go," said Beth. "You look so damned hot in it."

"Thank you, but I think you'll find me hot when it's off as well."

"You know I will."

Evie waited impatiently while Beth unhooked and unzipped the dress and helped her step out of it. Evie hung it up then turned to face Beth who was still in her tux.

"You're a little overdressed." Evie stepped out of her panties and lay naked on the bed.

"What? You're not going to help?"

"Do a striptease for me."

"Not going to happen."

Evie still watched in aroused pleasure as Beth stepped out of her clothes and joined her on the bed. They were lying skin to skin and Evie thought she would self-combust at the feeling of Beth's naked body against hers.

Beth kissed her and when their tongues met, Evie's world tilted on its axis. Beth brought her such pleasure both in and out of bed and she couldn't believe she was actually married to her. They were committed to each other for forever. The concept only heightened her arousal.

She grabbed Beth's knees with her thighs and rubbed up and down on it.

"You're so fucking wet," said Beth.

"I need to come."

"Happy to oblige."

Beth scooted down to where Evie's legs met. Evie spread as wide as she could. She needed the release only Beth could bring.

She felt Beth's mouth on her. Beth's no longer hesitant tongue moved in ways that Evie could not resist. She stroked every sensitive spot in Evie and on Evie and soon she could fight no longer. She pressed Beth's face into her as she felt the white heat shoot throughout her limbs and she rode the wave until she collapsed on the bed, spent.

"You've come a long way, babe," Evie said.

"Mm. Learning has been most enjoyable."

Evie laughed.

"You ready for me now?"

"I'm always ready for you."

Evie wanted to taste Beth's deliciousness, but knew Beth responded better to her fingers. So she plunged them deep inside her and stroked her silky insides before pulling them out only to delve further on the next thrust.

Soon Beth's ass was writhing on the bed, her eyes were closed, and Evie knew she was close. She dragged her fingers across Beth's clit, softly, teasingly, then pressed into it with meaning.

Beth rewarded her by tensing, crying out her name, and then relaxing like a noodle on the bed.

"Damn. I still can't get over what you do to me," Beth said.

"I do enjoy it."

Evie moved lower and lapped up the evidence of Beth's arousal. She moved her tongue along Beth's still twitching clit before licking inside her perfectly tight center. She was absolutely delectable and Evie could have stayed between her legs for the rest of eternity.

"Oh, fuck," moaned Beth. "You're going to make me come again."

Evie smiled to herself. That was indeed the goal.

Beth screamed again as she rode another orgasm and then weakly said, "No more."

Evie lay next to Beth, a place she'd come to cherish the past couple of years. She felt safe and happy, and most of all, home. She was where she belonged and where she would remain for the rest of her days.

Beth never ceased to amaze her. She was very proud of her for finishing her education. And was thrilled Beth hadn't needed her help to find a job. She'd found a position at a farm equipment manufacturing plant and was now a manager there. She didn't make as much as Evie, obviously, but she brought in a tidy sum and they lived more than comfortably.

They both missed Kelsey, but they video chatted at least once a week which eased the ache. Evie often checked in with Beth about living in a city when she'd grown up in such a rural setting, but Beth always assured her she was fine and that she actually felt more alive in Dallas.

Evie drifted off to sleep with these thoughts floating through her mind. She awoke late the next morning when a fully dressed Beth shook her shoulder gently.

"Babe? Wake up? We're supposed to meet Kels and Chris in an hour for brunch."

"What time is it?"

"Ten."

"Oh, shit. Why did you let me sleep so late?" But she wasn't angry. She felt more rested than she had in a very long time.

"You looked so peaceful and so beautiful that I couldn't bear the thought of waking you."

"You're so sweet. Join me?" She pulled the covers off and lay exposed for Beth's viewing pleasure."

"No time. Now, come on."

Brunch with Kelsey and Chris was a lot of fun. They went over details of the wedding, which was a good thing as it turned out none of them remembered everything. Each of them had committed something different to memory of their special day.

They hugged and said good-bye in the parking lot and vowed to keep up with their weekly chats. Then Evie and Beth got in their car and drove to Dallas to catch a flight to Akumal, Mexico, for their honeymoon on the Mayan Riviera.

Beth was quiet on the drive and Evie took her free hand.

"You okay?"

"Yeah. I'm fine."

"You're awfully quiet."

"Just kind of absorbing everything that's happened over the past couple of years," Beth said.

"There've been a lot of changes for you. You okay with that?"

"I'm great with them." Beth smiled at Evie. "Absolutely great."

"Good. Thank you for marrying me, Beth Richards."

"Thank you for marrying me, Evie Richards."

"I can't believe we're really married." Evie got the giggles.

"It's funny?" said Beth.

"Not funny. It just makes me giddy with happiness. I'm proud to be your wife."

"Good answer."

They drove in silence until Evie saw a sign for a rest stop.

"Please pull over when we get to the rest stop," she said.

"You need to use the restroom?"

"No. I need to have my way with you."

"In a rest area?"

"Why not? I want my wife and I shall have her. Anywhere I want. From now until eternity."

"I do like the sound of that." Beth pulled into the deserted rest area and Evie was grateful once again that she'd found her true soulmate in Beth.

About the Author

MJ Williamz is the author of twenty-one published novels and several dozen short stories. Three of their novels have been Goldie winners.

The desire to write struck young and has never gone away. From California's Central Coast to Northern California to Portland, Oregon to Houston, Texas, the need to put stories on paper has only grown and intensified.

MJ currently lives in Houston with their wife, fellow Bold Strokes Books author Laydin Michaels, three dogs and six cats.

Feedback? Feel free to reach out to mjwilliamz@aol.com.

Books Available from Bold Strokes Books

Catch by Kris Bryant. Convincing the wife of the star quarterback to walk away from her family was never in offensive coordinator Sutton McCoy's game plan. But standing on the sidelines when a second chance at true love comes her way proves all but impossible. (978-1-63679-276-7)

Hearts in the Wind by MJ Williamz. Beth and Evelyn seem destined to remain mortal enemies but are about to discover that in matters of the heart, sometimes you must cast your fortunes to the wind. (978-1-63679-288-0)

Hero Complex by Jesse J. Thoma. Bronte, Athena, and their unlikely friends, must work together to defeat Bronte's arch nemesis. The fate of love, humanity, and the world might depend on it. No pressure. (978-1-63679-280-4)

Hotel Fantasy by Piper Jordan. Molly Taylor has a fantasy in mind that only Lexi can fulfill. However, convincing her to participate could prove challenging. (978-1-63679-207-1)

Last New Beginning by Krystina Rivers. Can commercial broker Skye Kohl and contractor Bailey Kaczmarek overcome their pride and work together while the tension between them boils over into a love that could soothe both of their hearts? (978-1-63679-261-3)

Love and Lattes by Karis Walsh. Cat café owner Bonnie and wedding planner Taryn join forces to get rescue cats into forever homes—discovering their own forever along the way. (978-1-63679-290-3)

Repatriate by Jaime Maddox. Ally Hamilton's new job as a home health aide takes an unexpected twist when she discovers a fortune in stolen artwork and must repatriate the masterpieces and avoid the wrath of the violent man who stole them. (978-1-63679-303-0)

The Hues of Me and You by Morgan Lee Miller. Arlette Adair and Brooke Dawson almost fell in love in college. Years later, they unexpectedly run into each other and come face-to-face with their unresolved past. (978-1-63679-229-3)

A Haven for the Wanderer by Jenny Frame. When Griffin Harris comes to Rosebrook village, the love she finds with Bronte de Lacey creates safe haven and she finally finds her place in the world. But will she run again when their love is tested? (978-1-63679-291-0)

A Spark in the Air by Dena Blake. Internet executive Crystal Tucker is sure Wi-Fi could really help small-town residents, even if it means putting an internet café out of business, but her instant attraction to the owner's daughter, Janie Elliott, makes moving ahead with her plans complicated. (978-1-63679-293-4)

Between Takes by CJ Birch. Simone Lavoie is convinced her new job as an intimacy coordinator will give her a fresh perspective. Instead, problems on set and her growing attraction to actress Evelyn Harper only add to her worries. (978-1-63679-309-2)

Camp Lost and Found by Georgia Beers. Nobody knows better than Cassidy and Frankie that life doesn't always give you what you want. But sometimes, if you're lucky, life gives you exactly what you need. (978-1-63679-263-7)

Felix Navidad by 'Nathan Burgoine. After the wedding of a good friend, instead of Felix's Hawaii Christmas treat to himself, ice rain strands him in Ontario with fellow wedding-guest—and handsome ex of said friend—Kevin in a small cabin for the holiday Felix definitely didn't plan on. (978-1-63679-411-2)

Fire, Water, and Rock by Alaina Erdell. As Jess and Clare reveal more about themselves, and their hot summer fling tips over into true love, they must confront their pasts before they can contemplate a future together. (978-1-63679-274-3)

Lines of Love by Brey Willows. When even the Muse of Love doesn't believe in forever, we're all in trouble. (978-1-63555-458-8)

Manny Porter and The Yuletide Murder by D.C. Robeline. Manny only has the holiday season to discover who killed prominent research scientist Phillip Nikolaidis before the judicial system condemns an innocent man to lethal injection. (978-1-63679-313-9)

Only This Summer by Radclyffe. A fling with Lily promises to be exactly what Chase is looking for—short-term, hot as a forest fire, and one Chase can extinguish whenever she wants. After all, it's only one summer. (978-1-63679-390-0)

Picture-Perfect Christmas by Charlotte Greene. Two former rivals compete to capture the essence of their small mountain town at Christmas, all the while fighting old and new feelings. (978-1-63679-311-5)

Playing Love's Refrain by Lesley Davis. Drew Dawes had shied away from the world of music until Wren Banderas gave her a reason to play their love's refrain. (978-1-63679-286-6)

Profile by Jackie D. The scales of justice are weighted against FBI agents Cassidy Wolf and Alex Derby. Loyalty and love may be the only advantage they have. (978-1-63679-282-8)

Almost Perfect by Tagan Shepard. A shared love of queer TV brings Olivia and Riley together, but can they keep their real-life love as picture perfect as their on-screen counterparts? (978-1-63679-322-1)

Corpus Calvin by David Swatling. Cloverkist Inn may be haunted, but a ghost materializes from Jason Dekker's past and Calvin's canine instinct kicks in to protect a young boy from mortal danger. (978-1-62639-428-5)

Craving Cassie by Skye Rowan. Siobhan Carney and Cassie Townsend share an instant attraction, but are they brave enough to give up everything they have ever known to be together? (978-1-63679-062-6)

Drifting by Lyn Hemphill. When Tess jumps into the ocean after Jet, she thinks she's saving her life. Of course, she can't possibly know Jet is actually a mermaid desperate to fix her mistake before she causes her clan's demise. (978-1-63679-242-2)

Enigma by Suzie Clarke. Polly has taken an oath to protect and serve her country, but when the spy she's tasked with hunting becomes the love of her life, will she be the one to betray her country? (978-1-63555-999-6)

Finding Fault by Annie McDonald. Can environmental activist Dr. Evie O'Halloran and government investigator Merritt Shepherd set aside their conflicting ideas about saving the planet and risk their hearts enough to save their love? (978-1-63679-257-6)

Hot Keys by R.E. Ward. In 1920s New York City, Betty May Dewitt and her best friend, Jack Norval, are determined to make their Tin Pan Alley dreams come true and discover they will have to fight—not only for their hearts and dreams, but for their lives. (978-1-63679-259-0)

Securing Ava by Anne Shade. Private investigator Paige Richards takes a case to locate and bring back runaway heiress Ava Prescott. But ignoring her attraction may prove impossible when their hearts and lives are at stake. (978-1-63679-297-2)

The Amaranthine Law by Gun Brooke. Tristan Kelly is being hunted for who she is and her incomprehensible past, and despite her overwhelming feelings for Olivia Bryce, she has to reject her to keep her safe. (978-1-63679-235-4)

The Forever Factor by Melissa Brayden. When Bethany and Reid confront their past, they give new meaning to letting go, forgiveness, and a future worth fighting for. (978-1-63679-357-3)

The Frenemy Zone by Yolanda Wallace. Ollie Smith-Nakamura thinks relocating from San Francisco to her dad's rural hometown is the worst idea in the world, but after she meets her new classmate Ariel Hall, she might have a change of heart. (978-1-63679-249-1)

A Cutting Deceit by Cathy Dunnell. Undercover cop Athena takes a job at Valeria's hair salon to gather evidence to prove her husband's connections to organized crime. What starts as a tentative friendship quickly turns into a dangerous affair. (978-1-63679-208-8)

As Seen on TV! by CF Frizzell. Despite their objections, TV hosts Ronnie Sharp, a laid-back chef; and paranormal investigator Peyton Stanford, have to work together. The public is watching. But joining forces is risky, contemptuous, unnerving, provocative—and ridiculously perfect. (978-1-63679-272-9)

Blood Memory by Sandra Barret. Can vampire Jade Murphy protect her friend from a human stalker and keep her dates with the gorgeous Beth Jenssen without revealing her secrets? (978-1-63679-307-8)

Foolproof by Leigh Hays. For Martine Roberts and Elliot Tillman, friends with benefits isn't a foolproof way to hide from the truth at the heart of an affair. (978-1-63679-184-5)

Glass and Stone by Renee Roman. Jordan must accept that she can't control everything that happens in life, and that includes her wayward heart. (978-1-63679-162-3)

Hard Pressed by Aurora Rey. When rivals Mira Lavigne and Dylan Miller are tapped to co-chair Finger Lakes Cider Week, competition gives way to compromise. But will their sexual chemistry lead to love? (978-1-63679-210-1)

The Laws of Magic by M. Ullrich. Nothing is ever what it seems, especially not in the small town of Bender, Massachusetts, where a witch lives to save lives and avoid love. (978-1-63679-222-4)

The Lonely Hearts Rescue by Morgan Lee Miller, Nell Stark, Missouri Vaun. In this novella collection, a hurricane hits the Gulf Coast, and the animals at the Lonely Hearts Rescue Shelter need love, and so do the humans who adopt them. (978-1-63679-231-6)

The Mage and the Monster by Barbara Ann Wright. Two powerful mages, one committed to magic and one controlled by it, strive to free each other and be together while the countries they serve descend into war. (978-1-63679-190-6)

Truly Wanted by J.J. Hale. Sam must decide if she's willing to risk losing her found family to find her happily ever after. (978-1-63679-333-7)

A Good Chance by Ali Vali. Harry, Desi, and Desi's sister Rachel are so close to getting everything they've ever wanted, but Desi's ex-husband is coming back to get his revenge and rip apart their chance at happiness. (978-1-63679-023-7)

A Perfect Fifth by Jaycie Morrison. Streetwise pianist Zara Keller and Lady Jillian Stansfield couldn't be more different; yet their connection brings a new awareness of who they are and what they truly want in their lives—including each other. (978-1-63679-132-6)

Catching Feelings by Ana Hartnett Reichardt. Andrea Foster expected to catch a lot of pitches from the Alder Lion's star pitcher, Maya, but she didn't expect to catch feelings. (978-1-63679-227-9)

Defiant Hearts by Lee Lynch. In these stories, you'll find your lovers, friends, and lesbians you wish you knew—maybe even yourself. (978-1-63679-237-8)

Love and Duty by Catherine Young. All Princess Roseli wants is to marry her three lovers, but with war looming, she must instead marry Princess Lucia to establish a military alliance between their planets. (978-1-63679-256-9)

Murder at Union Station by David S. Pederson. Private Detective Mason Adler struggles to determine who killed a woman found in a trunk without getting himself killed in the process. (978-1-63679-269-9)

Serendipity by Kris Bryant. Serendipity brings jingle writer Annie Foster and celebrity pop star Bristol Baines together, and their undeniable attraction keeps them close, but will their different paths drive them apart? (978-1-63679-224-8)

The Haunted Heart by Jane Kolven. A ghost, a ring, and a quest to find a missing psychic—it's a spell for love. (978-1-63679-245-3)

The Rules of Forever by Nan Campbell. After reconnecting at their high school reunion, Cara and Lauren agree to embark on a textbook definition friends-with-benefits relationship, but trying to keep it uncomplicated is harder than it seems. (978-1-63679-248-4)

Vision of Virtue by Brey Willows. When virtue and desire come together, be prepared for sparks in this next installment of the Memory's Muses series. (978-1-63679-118-0)

Bold Strokes Books
Quality and Diversity in LGBTQ Literature